angel's secret

Gillian van der Walt

Just Done Productions
Publishing
Durban

First Edition 2012
ISBN: 978-1-920315-87-0

Just Done Productions
Publishing
Durban
2012

publish@justdone.co.za
http://www.justdone.co.za
International: http://www.Lulu.com/JustDone

Edited by Elaine Young

www.justdone.co.za

Acknowledgements

*F*irstly, I would like to thank my husband Tjaart for believing in me and egging me on to "keep writing". Without his support and the funding that goes into publication, I would not have come this far. I thank you from the bottom of my heart.

To my precious children Charlie, Wesley, Tyron and Nicole for allowing me the extra time to write, therefore being less available to attend to your needs. It's moments like these that I realise how blessed I am to have you and I love you all. Nicole my little princess now has her mommy back.

To the rest of my family and special friends – and I have many – you are my inspiration!

My sister Patricia Arnulphy – also my best friend – you play a big part in my life.

To Dina Grobbelaar, my friend and spiritual leader, you have an angelic soul.

To Moira York, I've known you for a short while but you've made things happen for me.

To Elaine Young, my Editor and my friend for your expertise and interest in my writing – you've given my books a home.

To Michele Swart, Natalie Marais, Dominique Smythe, Wendy Swanepoel and Jeannick Langeveldt who pre-read my manuscript and told me it was fab! You each played a part in reinforcing me, especially towards the end – you ran the race with me.

Leaving the best for last, I thank God for His grace in my life and all glory be to Him alone. It is my humble offering to bring good into the lives of others.

About the Author

Gillian van der Walt is married with four children and lives in Durban. Her previous book *Take my hand* is an autobiography.

Email her at: gillvanderwalt@gmail.com

www.gillvanderwaltauthor.co.za

For He shall give His angels charge over you, to keep you in all your ways. In their hands they shall bear you up, lest you dash your foot against a stone.
Psalm 91:11–12

You are about to step onto the road when something pulls you back just in time to avoid being hit by a speeding car. You are shocked. When you come to your senses, you ask yourself, "Could it be that an angel just saved me from a fatal accident?" I believe that angels walk with us. The verse tells us that God has given His angels charge over us to keep us in all our ways. And in their hands they will bear us up, so that not even a stone will trip us up.
Joseph Prince Ministries

Chapter 1

Angel woke up to the smell of her grandmother's baking. It was a smell that tantalised her tastebuds each and every time. Her Granny Jo always had a baking chore for her, and at only five years old Angel could whisk, beat and roll out dough like an expert. She loved those moments when they'd work side by side, chatting about all sorts of things.

But today Angel had a different request for her granny. Curious about the day she was born, Angel begged Jo to give her every last detail of the special event. At first Jo hesitated, then with a warm smile she went back in time.

'Beloved child...' she began, 'the day you were born was the best day of Granny's life. Your mommy was a very sick lady at the time. We prayed to Jesus and asked Him to keep you safe in her tummy until your time came to be born.' Angel listened raptly as Jo continued with her tale. 'Then that special day came and we were so happy when they told us you were a little girl.'

The smile on Angel's face grew wider. 'Was my mommy happy too?' she asked.

'Oh yes she was very happy, she even cried happy tears. But mommy was often sick, and that's when I would take you under my wing–'

'Granny, what does take me under your wing mean?' Angel interrupted.

Jo chuckled at her innocence. 'It means I took care of you when your mommy couldn't,' she replied.

'Tell me more Granny, go on!' the little girl begged.

Mustering up a bright voice, Jo continued with her tale. 'When I held you in my arms, I decided to name you Angel. Do you know why?' Angel shook her head. 'Because you were sent by Jesus. From that day on, you've been my little angel,' said Jo huskily, the emotion in her throat bringing the tale to an end. Then Jo told her one silly knock-knock joke after another, and they rolled out the rest of the cookie dough amidst squeals of laughter.

Though by no means well off, Jo voluntarily baked rusks, crunchies and koeksusters for the church, which she delivered every Monday afternoon. She had been brought up as a Christian, but had given her life to God fully when her daughter Sally had gone down a destructive path that brought her much pain.

Jo's husband Phillip had died at an early age and Jo had raised her daughter alone. Financially stricken, she had made do with a home that was more lower-class than middle-class, and had often felt guilty about denying her young daughter's needs. Jo had tried to keep Sally on the straight and narrow, but in time Sally had became involved in the wrong circle of friends. Before she knew it, drugs had become her source of daily 'joy'. Jo had cried many tears over her, and never quit praying. She knew God existed, and surely He would help her child when she couldn't.

By the age of twenty, Sally had fallen pregnant. Their world had come crashing down on them–or so it felt. The father of the child had been a one-night stand who Sally never saw again. For Jo, who had spent her life worrying about surviving, it felt like her life had come to an end. She had never hit rock bottom until that day when she felt it all too hard to bear. Financially struggling, with no husband for support and fighting a constant battle with her daughter's bad habits, she had wondered how they would manage a child too.

Sick with worry, Jo had resigned herself to her fate. But why, WHY...? she had wept daily, feeling like she was sinking deeper and deeper into a pit of gloom. It was at that time that someone had told her that her life was already written in God's book. And so was the child's. No child is ever a mistake for God, she was told. Jo wanted to know more; she needed to hear that there would be eventual light at the end of her dark, lonely tunnel.

That same week, she had turned to God in a desperate cry for help. She needed a miracle. The church became her refuge, and she found solace in learning more about God and His miracles. Over time, she learnt to accept Sally's choice of lifestyle without feeling guilty. Often she would sit at her kitchen table, staring out into the distance. She could see the church from her back door, and she would shake her head in disbelief that she had once looked upon that same church as an old building without any sense at all.

Sally's pregnancy was a dicey one from the beginning but God provided just enough for them. He had a plan for this unborn child, Jo knew it. Just weeks before Sally gave birth, the pastor of the church and his wife Cecilia paid Jo an unexpected visit. They arrived with bags of goods ranging from baby clothes to food parcels, nappies, a pram and a second hand crib. In an envelope was a generous donation which the congregation had collected in order to help Sally for the first few weeks of the baby's life.

Jo fell to her knees in sheer exhilaration. This was proof

that God was and is a merciful God who answers prayers. From that day, she volunteered to help in the church. Not only did she bake for all the special events, but she visited the sick and the lonely too.

The anticipated day of the birth finally arrived. The sunrise that morning was spectacular, as if God was sending his blessings through the sun's rays. Jo prayed all morning for her grandchild's safe and uncomplicated delivery. Sally had been on drugs from the age of fifteen, and Jo was worried that she may have continued during her pregnancy.

It was not until Sally's painful contractions began that she turned to her mother, as if reading her thoughts. 'Don't worry Mom, I've been clear of drugs for nine months,' she whispered. Jo let out a huge sigh of relief and said a silent prayer of thanks. Now she understood her daughter's extreme moodiness and intolerance during her pregnancy. Sally had remembered at least one good lesson she had taught her. It also showed that she cared for her unborn child.

After eight hours of intense labour and exhaustion, a healthy little girl was born. Sally hardly had the energy to look at her baby, let alone hold her, as she slipped in and out of reality. There was no mother-and-daughter bonding moment; instead Jo took her granddaughter into her arms, gazing lovingly into her eyes. *Thank you Father God for sending me Your Angel. You are so true to Your word and You always reward those who believe in You.* Jo had never lost her faith that God would protect both her daughter and grandchild.

Sally was happy with the name her mother had chosen: Angel. It had a good ring to it, she said with a shrug of her shoulder, as if to say *I wouldn't know what to call her so you can go ahead and do it for me.* Within days, Sally was back on her feet, partaking in drugs and alcohol once more. Jo tried to enforce motherly duties upon her, but she saw less and less of her daughter. For Jo, it felt like she had lost a daughter and gained another, like a second chance.

Angel brought meaning to Jo's life, and Jo channelled all her energy into being a super granny. She took each day as it came and never started it without giving thanks to God. Her pension money hardly made ends meet, but with help from the church and close friends, Jo and Angel never went without. 'Luxuries' had no meaning to them. They appreciated what was given to them and they learnt to be humble... although humble pie never tasted good.

Sally visited from time to time, but inevitably all the responsibility fell on Jo. When Angel was ready for pre-school, Jo could not afford uniforms or school shoes and so they were generously donated to her. By this stage Angel was old enough to know that she was different from her playmates. They all had their mommies to fetch them from school, and their daddies would lift them up onto their shoulders and treat them like princesses. It all seemed so surreal to her. She also felt left out because she never had pretty new clothes like the others. Attending birthday parties was not on Angel's list of favourites, and eventually she stopped being invited to most of them.

Jo would often overhear Angel having a conversation with her doll, pretending to be her sister and fantasising about a normal family life. And Jo allowed her to live in her make-believe world, knowing that it was those dreams that would open the door to greater things one day... in God's perfect time.

Chapter 2

*I*t was Angel's eighth birthday and she lay awake in her bed that morning, feeling excitement rise in her. The sun had already burned through the morning fog and in all the gardens, flowers bloomed.

'Happy Birthday Angel child!' shouted Jo joyfully, glancing about the messy room as she put a tray of breakfast down beside her. She leaned down to kiss her granddaughter on the cheek. 'Your mother and I have a special treat for you today, Madam. Wait till you hear about it…' teased Jo. They were taking Angel shopping for the first time, and she would get to choose her very own new dress. Under ordinary circumstances it would have been window shopping for Angel, who would squash her face up against the shop window and sigh longingly. This time she got to walk into the shop and browse to her heart's content.

'They're all so pretty, which one must I choose Granny?' Then she turned to her mom. 'Help me pick one Mommy'. After opinions were aired, Angel finally decided on a frilly pink and purple dress. 'Do we have enough money for this one?' she asked.

'It's your special day,' they both smiled. 'You don't have to look at the price tag today.'

Angel walked out of the store with a huge grin, hoping a

birthday invitation would soon come her way. A week later one did–from a girl named Alexis, who she had always envied for her beautiful dresses. Angel went to the party looking like Cinderella. Like fairy godmothers, the ladies from the church had braided her thin, blonde hair and painted her nails a pretty pink. As she walked through the door, the girls were astonished to see her dressed up.

But what was she to do now? Angel was shy and didn't dare follow the girls without being asked to. Sitting cross legged on the step, she watched them all play instead. After a while a little boy called her to play with his brand new red scooter. She didn't want to dirty her expensive dress so she chose to watch him instead. Clowning around on it and making *broom broom* sounds like a typical boy, he purposely kept falling off and sending her into fits of laughter. He loved the attention and after a while he came and sat down beside her.

'What's your name? Mine's Doug and I'm eight years old,' he said cheerily.

Angel bit her lip. 'It's Angel,' she said quietly. 'I'm eight too.' He was the friendliest boy Angel had ever met. As they talked, Angel learned that he was from up north and was visiting family for the holidays. She blushed when he told her she looked pretty in her dress.

Towards the end of the party as the children were leaving, Doug's father arrived to fetch him. As he staggered towards his son, Angel could see that he was drunk. She was annoyed to see how roughly he pulled Doug by the arm, hissing at him to 'hurry up and move along'.

'Wait Dad, I'm just saying goodbye to my friends,' Doug pleaded, and his father released him abruptly. They left a few moments later. This little boy was the only one who had spoken to her, let alone pay her a compliment. Dismayed at the tension between father and son, she wondered if his father always behaved that way.

That evening, the moon shone brightly through Angel's window. It had been an unusually warm day and the heat and humidity lingered in the house despite the open windows. Angel lay awake staring at the clusters of stars in the night sky. Jo had taught her how to pray, and each night they knelt together at her bedside to thank Jesus for the day's blessings.

Jo's greatest and most valuable lesson to Angel was about choices. One of her favourite Bible verses was from Deuteronomy 30:19, which says: 'Today I have given you the choice between life and death, between blessings and curses. Now I call on heaven and earth to witness the choice you make. Oh, that you would choose life, so that you and your descendants might live!'

'In any situation there is good and bad,' Jo would tell Angel. 'Life is all about making the right choices. You can choose life–celebrate it and be grateful for the least you have– or you can choose death, which is living in darkness, sin and self pity.' Jo had a way of turning each lesson into a story which was always the highlight of the evenings for Angel. Along with many valuable lessons learnt from her beloved grandmother, Angel knew that all bad situations were only temporary. Better days were to come, for those that believed.

But still there were times that Angel would break down and cry. Granny Jo was always there to lift her spirits and quote verses from the Bible. Another one of her favourite quotes was Psalm 139:13-15: 'For you created my inmost being; you knit me together in my mother's womb. I praise you because I am fearfully and wonderfully made; your works are wonderful, I know that full well.'

At the age of ten, Angel began to see God's miracles in her life. All the answered prayers and small mercies could come only from one source–Jesus. Once when Jo was sick with 'flu, Angel was panic-stricken that she would die. She was the only family Angel knew and she loved her with all her heart. So she knelt at her bed and prayed for God's healing upon her. Lo and behold, Angel woke up to Jo's singing the next day. She knew Jesus had heard her prayers.

When finances ran low, she would sometimes go to school without lunch, leaving the last few slices of bread for her grandmother. She would hear her granny run after her shouting, 'Angel... do you have your lunch packed in your bag?' 'Yes Gran, I have my lunch,' Angel would shout back. By that same afternoon, after hearing her prayer, Jesus had always provided for her. Someone would either share their lunch with her or she would find enough money on the floor to buy a hot dog or a pie.

Angel also prayed for her mother who was constantly in and out of rehab. She knew Sally couldn't kick her bad habits but never held a grudge against her. Instead Angel would look forward to each rare visit where they'd supposedly be a mother and daughter team.

Having to pretend that their time spent together was special made Angel feel guilty. She felt especially sick at the memory of their car rides home after her mother had been drinking. Each time her mother got drunk, it left another slash in the fabric of her life–a life of shadow with no substance. Still, Angel loved her unconditionally. The real mother she knew was standing in the kitchen, humming away as she baked rusks for the church.

Chapter 3

*F*our years went by and Angel grew into a responsible teenager. It was not easy being a teen in her part of town. She knew who the reckless no-goods were and stayed clear of them. Walking the streets after dark was looking for trouble. She had found that out two years previously when a man living down her street had followed her to school. He had tried to bribe her into taking drugs by offering her money, telling her that it could buy her an entire wardrobe of clothes. Trembling, she swallowed convulsively and fought for self-control. 'NO! I don't need your money and I don't want your stash!' she blurted out and ran as fast as her legs could carry her. There had been a few other hair-raising incidents but she had learnt to read the signs.

A week before her fourteenth birthday, Angel was invited to the movies with her classmates. Being asked to join them was an honour for her and she was madly excited. She had even saved up especially for the occasion. It took her almost two hours to get ready, but her heart sank when she looked in the mirror. With her limp, lifeless hair hanging on her shoulders, she looked thin and waif-like in her too-small clothes. Why do I have to grow up at all, she thought in despair. As always, Jo told Angel she looked beautiful. 'Oh Granny, you're only saying that 'cos you're my granny. You've never said an unkind word to anyone before,' Angel teased.

Jo laughed. 'My darling, nobody is perfect and one day someone will love you for who you are on the inside. Now hurry along and enjoy the evening with your friends. Laugh and be happy and forget about any self-doubt you may have.' Angel threw her arms around her gran and hurried to the door.

It was awfully windy outside and it had been raining for most of the day. Her heart beat in anticipation as she stood under the tree waiting for her lift to arrive. This was like a 'date' for her and it felt good to feel wanted. When her lift arrived, she was surprised to see that the car was full of fired-up teenage girls making a huge racket. She wondered how the father who was driving could possibly concentrate on the wet road. The rain was coming down in sheets and streamed across the windshield.

Sitting squashed at the edge of the seat against the door, Angel was nervous on the road for some reason that night. Perhaps because of the pelting rain or because she just felt out of place. Whatever that bad feeling was, she told herself to shake it off.

On finally arriving, the girls all got out of the car. Angel could not believe their fussing; they each shrieked about their hair getting wet and someone squealed because her shoes got muddy. Then two girls who were sharing one umbrella started to fight because the one had too much coverage. How irrelevant, Angel thought, thinking she too should fake some girlie squeal to fit the part. 'Ooooo, aaaah, look at my make-up, it's all running off my face,' she said in mock horror. 'Oh no... anyone have a tissue?' They all stopped and turned their gaze towards her. Was Angel wearing makeup? That would be a first! Feeling suddenly small, Angel said no more. Well at least that got them to stop fussing, she thought.

After faffing in the ladies' room for ages, the girls finally all walked down to the cinema to buy popcorn and Coke. When Angel reached the front of the queue, she was embarrassed to discover she didn't have enough money. So she just settled for the Coke, thankful that at least she had been invited out.

The movie was a romantic comedy that had Angel laughing out loud. Some of the comments weren't even funny but she was having such a great time that laughing just came naturally. It was only the third time she had ever been to the cinema. There were times when she could feel all eyes were upon her, but she didn't care.

Before she knew it, the movie had ended and all the girls rushed out towards the ladies' room again. *Oh no, not another powder-puff session*, thought Angel. She decided to wait outside for them. As she approached the bench nearby, she saw her neighbour running around frantically, searching for someone or something. Curious, Angel walked over to him and gently tapped him on the shoulder. 'Is everything okay Mr Stewart?'

He gave a huge sigh of relief on seeing her. 'Oh thank goodness I've found you,' he said. He stopped to take his breath as he was not a youngster anymore and she could see he had been running. 'Angel, I have some bad news....'

Angel froze. Was it her Granny or her mother? Just then Mr Stewart went on. 'Your mother has been in a car accident and is critical in hospital.' His words felt like a dagger through her heart. So that was the bad feeling that she had not been able to shrug off. She ran to find the other girls and yelled 'I'm leaving, there's been an emergency'. Then, bursting into tears, she ran after Mr Stewart to his car.

It was still raining heavily and she closed her eyes as they drove away, the silence heavy between them. Her Granny's words kept ringing in her ear: *Do not allow fear to grip you ever. Remember Psalm 23–'Even though I walk through the darkest valley, I will fear no evil, for you are with me; your rod and your staff, they comfort me.'*

Her gran's other favourite verse was Psalm 91:14-16 which said, *'"Because he loves me", says the Lord, "I will rescue him. I will protect him for he acknowledges my name. He will call on me, and I will answer him; with long life I will satisfy him and show him my salvation."'*

Arriving at the hospital, Angel ran straight into her granny's arms–the only arms she'd ever known around her. They felt safe and warm. Jo could not hide the sudden rush of tears. Angel wanted to soothe her pain. She had never needed to do that before; Jo had always been the strong one. Jo looked her granddaughter in the eye and tried to be strong as she explained what had happened.

'Angel, the accident was not your mother's fault, she had not been drinking this time. It was because of the wet roads that the car skidded and hit the barrier,' she said.

'Granny, will she survive the crash?' whispered Angel, frowning.

'Well, according to the doctor there is a very slim chance. God has a plan for her life Angel. Regardless what doctors say, if it is time for Him to have her back, it is not up to us.' Angel did not want to be strong, she just wanted to weep and never stop. This pain was so hard to bear, it even made her sick in the stomach.

'Granny, I don't feel very well…' cried Angel, clutching her tummy.

'It is normal, beloved child, and you may cry all you want. Granny's here for you,' Jo reassured her.

'I want to see her Gran, please let me see her,' pleaded Angel.

Jo nodded. 'Okay, but she may not respond and she is very weak, I must warn you.' She watched Angel through the window as she walked over to the bed and took her mom's hand in hers.

'Mommy, I know you can hear me. I just want to say that this accident was not your fault Mommy. This time you are not blamed for this.' Angel paused for a moment, trying to compose herself. 'I love you Mom and I know you love me too. I wish we had spent more time together.' She stopped and paused for another moment. 'The little I knew of you was enough to make me happy Mommy.'

Angel saw a tear falling from her mother's eye. Wiping the tear from her cheek, Angel bent over and kissed her hand. Angel knew her mom had heard and understood. She was relieved knowing that she had told her that she loved her… for the first time in fourteen years. *Thank you Jesus for giving me this one chance to say it to her*, Angel said silently in her heart. She kissed her hand again and walked out.

For three days Sally remained in a coma. Every day Jo and Angel visited with new flowers picked from their little garden. Angel was no longer devastated. Instead she felt a warm, peaceful presence every time she entered the room. If God were to take Sally, she would not be angry. She realised that her life with Jesus was far more rewarding than the life she had been living, in and out of pubs.

On the third day Sally took her final breath. She went peacefully and in the presence of her loved ones. With gathering tears, Angel stood at the foot of the bed. It was mind boggling for her, witnessing death for the first time… let alone her own mother's. She was concerned about Jo's sobbing more than anything. This was not like her strong gran. But Sally was her only child after all, and she had loved her with all her heart.

That night sleep did not come easily for Angel, although she was exhausted from all the emotion. She drifted in and out of dreams, and awoke in the early hours of the morning to the sound of loud music coming from down the road. They always had parties till all hours of the morning. There were often times when she would hear the police sirens too, never quite knowing the reason why. She climbed into bed with her gran and she heard her talking to God. Hearing her praying was comforting for Angel. Immediately sleep came to her and that's where she spent the night, warm and safely tucked at the side of the only mother she now had – and the mother she had always been.

Chapter 4

As the months dragged by, Jo became noticeably weaker. She was normally stalwart and steady but now Angel thought she looked far older than her sixty-seven years. Her arthritis got a lot worse as the weeks passed, and they could no longer go for their usual walks. Even the baking became less. Angel knew that if they had more money, they would be able to afford the proper medication for Jo. Without it, Jo had to get used to hobbling slowly with a walking stick. The only real outing she had was to church, and occasionally to get groceries.

Angel found it an all-consuming job to run after Jo and keep up with her own school work. She never asked anyone for help but she humbled herself to accept any and every offer given to her. By the time Angel reached her eighteenth birthday, Jo had become very frail. Her best friend Cecilia from church was very concerned about her and suggested that Angel put her in a home with proper care.

'No that is not necessary Aunt Cecilia. I will take care of my gran as I have no-one else to see to,' Angel insisted. She devoted all her extra time to her most loved gran in the world. And night after night, despite her frailty, Jo lectured to Angel about 'life lessons'. She was afraid that Angel would be abandoned if she were to die. Besides her good neighbour and loyal friends from church, Angel knew no-one.

Angel was very mature for her age and quite independent. She was determined to study at varsity one day but she also knew that she would need to work first and earn the money for her studies. She had it all worked out. At the end of her final school year, Angel passed with distinction. Jo was so proud of her, and the ladies from the church decided to throw her a surprise party at home. Jo agreed to it and was most happy for them to take over her little abode. But she did warn them that her legs could not carry her and that they would need to do the setting up. The house was filled with a buzz of good cheer all afternoon, and nothing could have made Jo happier.

Late that afternoon, on arriving home from her final day of school, Angel waltzed up the path to the front door. She had no inkling whatsoever of what was about to come her way. As she unlocked the door and stepped in ready to shout 'Gran, I'm home', she heard the loudest, most festive cheer ever. 'SURPRISE...!' shouted a chorus of women's voices. The look on her face was priceless. She had never been given a surprise celebration in her life. Giddy with congratulations and warm compliments, Angel beamed throughout the evening. Oh she so needed to hear those words of affirmation, and she was so thankful for her grandmother's friends for their special care.

The magical evening finally came to an end and Angel waved the last car off as midnight struck. After tucking in her frail granny, Angel fell asleep with a smile on her face. The evening had belonged to her. She was proud for having made it this far without a single day of losing hope.

Christmas was around the corner. It was never a big affair in her home. Each year Angel and Jo would stay awake until midnight and exchange gifts next to the Christmas tree.

'Gran, what do you want for Christmas this year? And don't tell me slippers 'cos you are hardly walking anymore. Give me a hint of what your heart really desires,' she teased. 'Oh and don't say chocolates either–you always share them with me and I end up finishing them all,' Angel giggled.

'I know what I want this Christmas,' said Jo as she gazed at Angel. 'It's for you to promise me that when I am no longer on this earth, you will always make sure that you put up a tree and decorate it. No matter how lonely one gets, Christmas is a time of hope and it lifts the spirits.' Angel looked at her with puppy dog eyes. 'Oh and don't forget what goes on the very top of the tree high above the rest...' Jo added, choking with emotion.

'Yes Gran... I know what goes on the top... ME, your angel.' Since Angel had been old enough to decorate the tree, Jo had always told her that she was her Angel on the top. Those words had made her giggle and blush–year after year. 'Okay, I promise you Gran, you can count on me. But that is not enough, what else do you want? There has to be something,' pressed Angel as she grabbed her cup of hot chocolate and snuggled against Jo.

Jo needed to think quickly of a very inexpensive gift, knowing that Angel could not afford it. 'Alright alright... you can give me a box of Turkish Delight. In that way, it will all be mine because I know you don't like them,' said Jo, laughing.

Christmas Eve arrived and they erected the Christmas tree in Jo's room next to her bed. They played Christmas songs and tried to stay awake, but by 10.30pm they were both sound asleep. Cleverly, Angel had set an alarm for 11.50pm. This must have been the first year that they had failed to keep awake. They jumped at the sound of the alarm and happily exchanged gifts at midnight. They could hear the echoes of celebration coming from the neighbours.

Jo's gift to Angel was different this year. It was a small red box tied with a golden ribbon. It looked expensive and sentimental. When Angel opened it she gasped in excitement. It was Jo's exquisite engagement ring. Her grandpa Phillip had been the son of a wealthy man and had lavished Jo with expensive gifts and jewellery when they were first married. Then a family feud had arisen which caused much heartache amongst the family and led to Phillip's parents disowning him. Over the years, Jo had treasured her jewellery as a reminder of her husband–until she had had to pawn off a piece at a time to pay for Sally's rehabilitation. Eventually all she had left was her engagement and wedding ring.

'Gran, I don't know what to say.... I... I will treasure this forever Granny,' Angel choked, happy tears trickling down her face. She hugged her grandma tightly in her arms.

'You are welcome my darling. I will hang on to my wedding ring for now if you don't mind. I cannot break my wedding vows, you know. I promised "to love and to cherish ' til death us do part". I still carry your grandpa in my heart, you know. He was such a good man,' said Jo. 'But promise me that you will remember to take it when I close my eyes. The set belongs to you and you mustn't let go of it until your daughter turns eighteen one day. Only then may you pass it on to her.'

'Of course Gran, I will treasure it–it symbolises true love, like love from a fairy-tale book,' said Angel softly.

Jo took her hand. 'One day you too will find love and he–.' But Angel cut her sentence off quickly.

'Oh I don't think so Gran. No man would want to look my way, I'm really nothing on the outside,' said Angel with her head facing the floor.

Jo cupped her cheek. 'Angel, don't say that. I've told you

before, a true man will see what is inside of you. He will fall in love with that beauty so radiant and full of passion. A woman's character matters greatly in a marriage. He would be a fool not to see you for the angel you are.'

Her gran's reprimand, though spoken gently, had struck hard. 'Thank you so much Gran... but I think you need to get to bed now,' said Angel, getting up to tuck Jo into bed. 'Thank you for another wonderful Christmas spent with the best gran in the world.' She went back to her room, got down on her knees and whispered, *Happy birthday Jesus. You are the only Father I've ever had and I love You for all my blessings. Thank you....* Then she tucked herself in, cast one last look at the diamond ring on her bedside table, and fell into a blissful sleep.

Chapter 5

*A*fter the Christmas holidays, Angel was on a mission to look for work. She was willing to do anything, even pack groceries if it meant earning some money. Weeks of job searching went by, and she prayed that she would soon be successful. In February of the New Year, she was finally offered a job in the bank. She had passed matric with honours and was thrilled at the prospects of working in the lucrative world of banking.

Hardly able to contain her excitement, she ran into the room where her gran lay sleeping. A glimpse of afternoon sun was beaming through the curtain. 'Gran, Gran, wake up, I have great news...' she squealed as she gently shook her gran awake.

Jo opened her eyes, which looked heavy and tired. 'Did you get the job my child?' she whispered.

Angel nodded vigorously, clapping her hands. 'Yes Gran and the money is good. I will be able to save AND spoil us at home. I will buy that expensive coffee you love and more Turkish Delights and–' Angel stopped as her gran's head sank to the side of the pillow. She had a smile on her face but her eyes were closed again, and she was far too quiet and still.

'Gran, are you sleeping? Gran, wake up please...' pleaded Angel anxiously. Sick with dread, she took her gran's hand in her own. It felt warm but limp... and immediately she knew that her worst nightmare had come true. Her granny was gone forever, safely in Jesus' arms. Her lip quivered and she wept inconsolably. 'Oh Granny, oh my Granny... I love you so much. Go and be with Mom, she needs you now.' Angel kissed her on the lips and covered her face with her warm blanket. Jo had held out until she knew that Angel had found a job to support herself. Now she could let go. Now SHE would be the Angel watching over her granddaughter.

The days that followed were no easy task. Angel needed to stop the tears that never seemed to run low. Her gran's death was far more painful than her mom's had been. It was nothing less than torture. She didn't eat for three days and was sleep deprived. Aunt Cecilia opened her home to Angel until she was able to support herself fully. Angel thanked her and asked her for some time to reply to her kind gesture. After long thought, she decided to stay on at the house—on her own. It was paid off and Jo had left the house in her name. It was the only thing she had to give, besides her wedding band which Angel now clung onto for dear life.

The morning of her first day at work required great courage. She had to walk to the bus stop in heels, which she had not practised beforehand. By the time she got there she already had blisters. Then she had to walk another few blocks from the middle of the CBD to the bank itself. When she finally reached work, she headed straight for the ladies' room to freshen up. Grieving in the silence, she could still hear Jo speaking to her in that firm but gentle voice: *Angel, remember the choices you have: to give up or to make the best of every difficult situation. Life or death. Choose life Angel, and hold your head up high. You can do this my girl. I have no doubt whatsoever.* Angel looked around her as if to look for Jo—but she was the angel on her shoulder. Jesus was on the other shoulder. Instantly, she was filled with a sense of peace and calm. She stood tall and smiled her way in to work. To look at her, one would never say she had just lost the one and only good thing in her life.

Chapter 6

*A*ngel adapted to her new job and loved what she did. Having no other obligations, she spent most of her time at work, even volunteering to work every Saturday. Weekends at home were her worst. Besides the odd visit from certain church friends or the occasional outing, she was at home alone with Jo's big furry cat, Mimi. She was not an animal lover but just the thought of not being completely alone in the house was reassuring. At times, Mimi would stare at her as if to say, 'I know you're lonely, but I can be of good company to you'.

A year went by without Angel missing a single day at work. She managed to save money and invest it in a fixed deposit, ready for that special day when she would draw all her hard-earned cash to pay for her studies. Working with less fortunate people was her passion and she was determined to study psychology. To be an educational psychologist might be an even better choice, given her love of children. But she had plenty of time to decide and make sure that she was not making the wrong career choice.

Christmas was drawing near again and she partially dreaded it. It had no meaning without Granny Jo. She had been invited to a pre-Christmas party but she was not in the right frame of mind. She felt uncomfortable around 'happy couples'. Soon to turn twenty-one, she had never had a relationship with a guy. She didn't know how it felt to be hugged or told that she was special. Whenever these thoughts crossed her mind, she would quickly block them out. She remembered her gran's words: *Angel, it is so easy to let yourself go. Don't allow yourself to fall into that pit of despair and sadness. It will only make you dwell on all your little misfortunes. The devil wants to take you down, he wants you to give up so that he can win you over. But be one up on him and count your blessings. They may be few but there are others worse off than you. One day, God will give you back blessings and happiness tenfold.* With those warm thoughts and very wise words, Angel rolled up her sleeves and got stuck into her pre-Christmas baking.

Angel worked as a consultant with another young lady of a similar age. Crystal was her name and she was rather temperamental–there were days when Angel wouldn't dare even look in her direction. She seemed to have problems with her boyfriend. When the grumpy look appeared on her face, Angel knew to stay clear as it meant another argument had taken place. At times Angel tried to question her about the reason behind the moods, but she soon learned to do as she was told–'butt out'.

Every Friday there was a buzz in the office. Everyone was in a happy mood as they planned their weekend. Angel loved to hear all the different stories and plans they made, though they all sounded far too busy. The women with children made her think twice about having little kiddies one day–where would her precious time go to? After work on a Friday, they would all congregate in the canteen which also had a pub. She had never once joined them in the year she had worked there. One day Crystal urged her to come along. 'Come on Angel, you need to get a life and join us this time. You won't meet anyone if you keep hiding yourself,' she said. 'Come with me and I'll introduce you to the people in this building you've never met before.'

Somewhat indecisively, Angel agreed. 'Alright, why not. But could you give me a lift home? I don't want to walk in the dark.'

'Of course, that's the least of your worries. Now come on, let's show you how to have a good time,' said Crystal enthusiastically.

On arriving at the canteen, Crystal introduced her to a few people. Then she disappeared into the crowd, leaving Angel to sit alone at the bar. It wasn't surprising–Crystal was an attractive girl and all the guys liked her. She knew it too, and did a good job of flaunting it in front of them. Her personality seemed erratic at times to Angel: she could be all chatty, flirty and loud in public, yet when alone with Angel, she had a sweet, quiet side to her. Angel silently thanked God that she did not have that kind of pressure on herself. It must be hard work being constantly in the limelight.

When Angel stepped into the ladies' room a little later, she could hear someone crying. It sounded muffled but it was definitely coming from the cubicle next to her. It was not her place to ask who it was or if they needed help, so she left it and quietly walked out. But she lingered at the door, curious to see who it was. After what felt like forever, Crystal walked out. Angel had thought as much and wondered if she had had another fight with her boyfriend Colin.

'Crystal, there you are. I was looking for you, is everything okay?' Before Crystal could reply, she burst into tears. Angel gave her a warm hug and led her outside to get some air. Then Crystal started to tell her the reason for her tears, and Angel just listened. It's what Crystal needed–someone to listen. It turned out that she was being physically and emotionally abused by Colin. He had such control over her that she felt powerless under his evil grip. She never showed her bruises and was a master at hiding them.

Crystal had been drinking that night. Angel guessed that she wouldn't be happy with herself the next day for having revealed her ugly truth to someone like her. 'I wish I knew what to say to you Crystal,' she began. 'I've got no experience when it comes to love but I don't know why you are allowing him to do this to you–.' Before she could finish her sentence, Crystal cut her short.

'Oh I did not ask you to preach to me or fix my problems. Just forget I ever spoke to you,' Crystal said curtly before storming off, leaving Angel feeling very remorseful about what she had said.

Angel spent the rest of the evening watching everyone in great detail. The music was good and she just wanted to get up and dance. It amazed her how the prettier girls got the attention. Yet the girls with partners or wedding rings seemed the most content. That's what she longed for–to be loved for HER, not her looks.

At the end of the evening, Crystal signalled Angel that she was leaving. The silence in the car cut like a knife and Colin drove like a maniac. Hoping that they would not have a squabble until she arrived home safely, she was relieved when they stopped in front of her house. She could not really tell if Crystal was still mad with her but thanked her anyway. 'See you on Monday' she shouted as Colin sped off so fast that his tyre marks would probably be engraved in the tar forever.

She walked towards her gate. To her left was a group of drunkards lying all over the pavement. To her right a woman was hitting a man with her handbag, clearly angry at what he had done. He kept laughing and Angel knew this would infuriate the girl even more, but she didn't care to look twice. She got in and locked the door behind her.

She thought back to the happy couples and how they had danced together and looked so perfectly made for each other. When would her turn come? Would she be lucky enough to find someone she could trust? Climbing into bed, she stared at the engagement ring, wondering when her Mr Right would come along and turn the ugly duckling into a beautiful, radiant swan.

Chapter 7

Monday finally came. Angel needed to occupy her mind with her work in order to chase away the 'make believe' dreams in her head. She was not expecting to have a good day with Crystal and was pleasantly surprised when she approached her. 'Angel, I just want to say thank you for caring on Friday night. I had no right to speak to you that way.' Crystal paused for a moment. 'At times I don't realise what I say – perhaps I have an anger problem.'

Angel looked at her sympathetically. 'Don't apologise Crys. I think you react that way because you're tired of being controlled.' Crystal was quiet. 'I wish there was something I could do to help you, but until you ask me I will keep my distance. So for now, let's just talk work, okay?' With a gentle smile, Angel held her hand out to her.

Crystal took her hand and looked up at Angel. 'There's something about you Angel, something angelic. It's good to know I have someone like you close by.' As the two girls hugged, they were interrupted by their Department Manager, Mr Reid. He called Angel into his office. It made her blush. She had never been called into an office before and felt like a bad girl.

'Take a seat Angel,' said Mr Reid as he sat at the opposite end of his desk. 'According to your records, I see that you have never taken leave or missed a single day's work.' In the silence of the small room, she could hear the pounding of her heart. 'In a month's time, you will have been in this company a full year,' he continued. 'I hope that you will be taking leave to spend some time with your family and loved ones,' he said. Mr Reid had no idea that home and family life were non-existent for her.

'Yes Sir, I realise that. I will certainly be taking leave soon. Thank you for pointing that out to me and having my best interests at heart,' she replied with relief. Mr Reid dismissed her with a polite smile. She was thankful she had a caring boss, unlike many others out there. Some would never dream of reminding their employees that they had leave due to them.

A week before Christmas as Angel lay on the bed staring blankly into space, Jo's words rang in her ears: *Promise me that you will still put up the tree and decorate it.* Angel was still mourning her gran terribly but she knew she needed to face that moment. Quickly she stood up, robot-like, and reached up to the top of the wardrobe to grab the box where the tree was kept. Not only did the box come flying down with a bang, but also a cockroach and his entire family too. Angel gave a loud screech and the cat jumped off the bed and hid behind the curtain. Angel hated roaches. What good was it to scream when no-one would come running to her rescue anyway, she thought. She ran to find the Doom spray but it was empty. *Aaargh!* she thought and shooed away the roaches with a broomstick before she touched the tree.

She turned on the Christmas carols and started decorating. Strangely, she was not sobbing or distraught; instead she felt that same peace come over her that she had felt on her first day at work. 'Is that coming from you Gran?' she spoke out loud. 'Did you ask Jesus to give me strength? If you did, it really is working. I can do this Gran, I can do this for US, you and me. I miss you but you are here; I can feel your presence.'

She had just finished the tree when the phone rang, causing her to jump. It was Aunt Cecilia. 'Hello Angel darling. I know that you're alone at home, so please would you join us for dinner this Christmas Eve?' she asked.

'Yes Aunt Cecilia, nothing would please me more,' Angel replied, beaming. She was happy not to face Christmas Eve alone. Besides the need to be distracted, she also needed a good nutritious meal. She hated cooking for herself, and although she could afford to buy cooked meals, she often forgot to stop at the shops.

Standing in front of the mirror on Christmas Eve she once again saw the pale, thin, unattractive girl with dull hair, no makeup and no sense of style. There seemed to be no point in wearing makeup. Her hair badly needed cutting and styling, as Crystal constantly reminded her, and her body needed some fattening up. Luckily she was now able to buy decent clothes that fitted her. She did what she could to touch up her appearance until she heard the car outside. It was Aunt Cecilia. Excitedly, Angel locked up and drove off for her special evening out.

Aunt Cecilia had a few guests over that night, and they were all happy, friendly people. They came to greet Angel and not the other way round. A little girl sitting alone in the corner immediately caught her attention. 'Hey there gorgeous one, my name is Angel. What is yours?' Angel asked as she approached her cautiously. But the little girl just stared at her and did not reply. Thinking she was just shy, Angel continued, 'I bet it's a very pretty name, can I have three guesses?' The timid girl nodded shyly.

'Mmm let me guess, is it Nicole?' She shook her head. 'Is it Teaghan perhaps?' Again she shook her head. 'Ah, it must be Melissa then?' she teased, but again she shook her head.

'I'll tell you what, don't worry to tell me your name just yet. I will soon find out. In the meantime, would you like to come with me for a walk outside?' Without hesitation the little girl stood up and took her hand. As happy as Angel was that she had accepted her offer, she was also curious about why she didn't want to speak.

It was the perfect, still night, full of stars that lit up the sky. Angel did not press the subject of speaking with the little girl but instead started to tell her a Christmas story. They must have been outside for almost an hour when the girl's mother came out calling her name. 'Katie, I need to know if you are outside, please raise your hand if you are, so that I can see you,' she said in a slightly panicked voice. Both Angel and Katie's hands went up and Angel was pleased that she now knew the little girl's name. Her mom came out to join them. 'Hi, my name is Faith and you are...?'

Angel shook her hand. 'I am Angel. Aunt Cecilia was my gran's best friend,' she said.

'Yes I've heard about you,' Faith replied. 'Aunt Cecilia speaks highly of you. She says you're a strong, courageous girl.' She smiled at Angel. 'I am sorry at the loss of your gran.' Leaning down to kiss her daughter on the cheek, Faith continued. 'As you may have noticed, Katie refuses to speak. Our home was destroyed in a fire last year and her father ran in to save her but didn't make it out. Since then she hasn't spoken. We have tried everything from doctors to therapy...'

Faith looked so forlorn that Angel's heart was torn. She hated to see people suffer, let alone little innocent children. After a long chat, Faith went inside and Angel turned Katie's chin in her direction. 'One day you WILL speak again but right now, all that matters is that I'm spending time with you and I am so glad that we are friends,' Angel said softly to her, trying to be strong. Katie reluctantly shifted closer to her and

Angel gave her a big hug.

The evening was festive and Angel really enjoyed the company. Cecilia had offered for her to spend the night but Angel preferred to be home, near the Christmas tree which she had erected next to Gran's bed. She got home just before midnight. Grabbing the angel and reaching up to the top of the tree, she gently placed it there. She could visualise Jo's smile in the mirror of her eyes. 'Merry Christmas Granny,' she said aloud. 'I've no doubt you are having a feast with Jesus on His birthday. I love you Gran and I will always miss you, but you will always be a part of me.' Then she went onto her knees and said a prayer.

Happy birthday Jesus. Thank you for an evening of great joy. This little girl Katie needs You Lord. She is very confused and hurt and it appears that she has not found the right person to help her heal. Please allow me to try. Give me a sign of what You want me to do. So many people out there are hurting Lord. Please use me and tell me how I can empower their lives. As for me, I am content Lord. My strength comes from You, and the peace that flows in me enables me to live each day. I love and trust You and I know You have a plan for my life. I will wait upon You. Amen. Angel climbed into bed alongside her ginger cat and they both fell asleep to the sweet sound of crickets chirping outside her window.

Chapter 8

On Boxing Day Angel woke up to the sound of her alarm going off at five thirty. Usually she woke up before the alarm went off, but this morning she felt awfully tired. Then it suddenly came to her. She had just dreamt the most beautiful dream a girl could ever ask for. In her dream, she had been transformed into a new person. She was beautiful and elegant with long, shining, dark hair and a lovely colouring to her glowing skin. Her nails were manicured and she wore the most gorgeous of dresses. Everywhere she went, eyes would follow her. When she woke up and realised that it was nothing but a good dream, she was faintly disappointed and wished the illusion could have gone on forever. *Why this dream?* she wondered. It was not like her to dream unless she was sick.

She sat up in bed for a while longer, with glimpses of the dream going over and over again in her mind. Then a feeling came over her that told her that this had been no mere dream; it was God-sent. In her prayer last night she had asked God to use her in order to help others. But how could this possibly help them?

For the rest of Boxing Day, she lazed around. Not realising that it was not the usual work day, she had forgotten to switch off her alarm the previous night. Her neighbourhood was festive once again with music blaring from as early as lunch time, and she knew it would probably go on until midnight.

As low class as they were, Angel's neighbours never really gave Angel a hard time; instead they would watch over her house, knowing she was alone most of the time. She too was never rude to them but knew to leave them alone. It wasn't worth complaining–it was their way of life and she was used to it.

Two days into the New Year, Crystal invited Angel to her twenty-first birthday party. She could not turn down the only friend she had. They had grown closer over the past few months and Angel knew to overlook her weaknesses. Often Crystal would phone her late at night to chat and ask her opinion about things. It gave Angel a sense of need. 'Thanks Crys, of course I will be there and no, I do not have a partner so you did not have to write "Dear Angel and partner" on the invitation,' said Angel pulling a tongue at her friend.

Crystal giggled. 'I asked the fairy godmother to send you one for the night so let's see what happens,' she chuckled, giving Angel a friendly nudge before carrying on with her work.

During that week, Angel heard all about the preparations for the party and how Crystal was looking to invite a hundred people. By the end of the week, Angel wished the party was over with and life could return to normal. She did go shopping for the special occasion though. Having bought herself enough clothes lately, she chose a beautiful scarf instead. Its gorgeous colours and silky texture complemented her black dress and silver earrings perfectly.

Catching the bus early that afternoon, she hoped to be the first to arrive in order to help Crystal set up. Crystal had already had a few drinks by the time Angel arrived and this could mean trouble. She knew too well from her mom's days how quickly one can get slaughtered. 'Happy birthday Crys, your day has finally come!' said Angel as she embraced her friend.

Crystal was in a happy mood. Angel was relieved as this meant that she could warn her about taking it slow with the wines without making her angry. Whenever Angel wanted to warn her about something or make an honest judgement, she needed to check first if she was in her happy mood. If she wasn't, it could have disastrous effects. 'Hey, easy on the wine, the night is yet a puppy so let's get you some water,' said Angel as she yanked her friend into the kitchen. She didn't want her friend to embarrass herself on her special night.

Among the latecomers was a friendly guy who waltzed in as if he owned the place, gave everyone a hug and went straight to the fridge for a drink. A few minutes later, he pulled up a chair next to Angel. 'I see you're left to sit all alone, that's no good,' he said, grinning. She turned and smiled at him.

'I don't mind sitting alone. I love watching people, it amuses me,' she said.

For a moment he stared at her with his head tilted slightly to one side. 'Nice scarf, it really suits your dress,' he said, leaving Angel stunned. Relief flooded her–someone had noticed and approved! But was he genuine or was it just a pick-up line? For the first time she didn't care either way. He had noticed her scarf when no-one else had–plus she had never been flirted with by any guy before, and she felt a bubble of excitement at the thought.

They ended up chatting about odds and ends and she enjoyed his great sense of humour. But as the evening went on, she noticed he had had a little too much to drink. His hazy, heavy eyes and slurring speech were no longer attractive to Angel. Instead, she became agitated and wished he would just get lost. He kept moving around from group to group but always came back to her as if he had booked the chair beside her all for himself. Why did he keep coming back to her? Did he like her or did he like the fact that she listened to all his garbage? After speeches were said and dinner had been served, everyone got up to dance. By that time, he was swaying to and fro. He asked her to dance, but she refused. When he asked why, she replied, 'Because you would probably stand on my toes or fall over me.'

He blushed. 'Next time then, when I'm a good boy.' And with that he turned and walked away. Angel suddenly felt awkward about having said something so bold. Finding him outside on the steps, she saw him put his head in his hands. Unsure whether to sit next to him or not, she made her way over to where he was sitting.

'Hey, you okay? I didn't mean to offend you,' she said shyly.

'That's fine, you didn't offend me. I'm the jerk that never seems to learn,' he muttered and with that, walked off in the direction of his car.

'Hey, I didn't get your name...' she called after him.

'Doug, my name is Doug,' he shouted back. And then he was gone.

Angel sat on the step for a while longer hearing his name over and over... Doug. Could it be... no it couldn't. She had never forgotten the friendly little boy who had told her she was pretty. It seemed strange that this Doug was just as friendly and had also complimented her. Pity about his drinking though. If it weren't for that, she could say that she had enjoyed every minute of her evening. Doug... Doug.... The name kept repeating in her head as well as her heart.

Chapter 9

ngel could not wait for the following Monday to ask Crystal about Doug. For some odd reason, she could not get him off her mind all weekend.

'Hey Crys...' Angel said as they walked out together for lunch break. 'So tell me more about Doug.' Crystal looked at her curiously.

'Oh yes, I saw you two talking to each other at the party. Well, all I can tell you is that he's a nice guy, but unfortunately he has a drinking problem and he's scared off many girls in the past. No girl wants a boozer as a boyfriend; and to make it worse, he gets aggressive towards the end of the evening. We've seen it many times,' said Crystal as she bit into her sandwich. Angel nodded and didn't ask any more questions. She didn't want to go down that road again. Alcoholism had been part of her childhood and she hated the sad memories it brought back.

That evening she had a longing to see Katie again. She had promised the sweet little girl a visit but had been so busy preparing for the party that she hadn't had a chance. Reaching for the phone, she dialled Faith's number and asked her to put Katie on the phone. Faith was pleased and asked Angel to hold while she called Katie. Angel could hear Faith telling her who it was. Then Faith came back on. 'Angel, you can talk now, Katie is ready to listen,' she said.

Angel began to talk. 'Hello Katie, it's me Angel. I thought I would phone to say that I have not forgotten my promise to visit you. I've been a little busy lately. If you would still like me to visit then tap the mouthpiece of the phone twice.' She hadn't rehearsed this and prayed that Katie would respond. *Tap, tap*, she heard on the other end of the line. 'Thank you Katie, then I will be at your place on the weekend. I have a surprise for you. Now you go off to bed and have sweet dreams. I can't wait to see you again,' she said. She paused for a moment and hoped that Katie had been listening. 'I will say goodbye now so if you tap three times then I know you're saying goodbye too, okay?' Angel waited until she heard three taps. Then she hung up, feeling a special warmth inside her–this little girl had really crept into her heart. Angel waited in anticipation for the weekend to come.

After work the following day, Angel sat at the bus stop reading her book. She wasn't one to take notice of the people walking past or sitting next to her. She had just opened her book and started reading when she heard a familiar voice.

'Hello again, fancy meeting you here. What are you doing at a bus stop?' It was Doug. Her heart skipped a beat and she almost dropped her book. She immediately presumed that she looked like a drag after a full day's work.

'Hi Doug, now that I know your name. Good to see you again.' She suppressed a smile. 'What brings YOU to a bus stop? Is your car being serviced?' she asked, unable to calm the wild beating of her heart.

'Well... it's at the panel beaters at the moment. I had a small accident the other day but nothing serious,' he replied, then changed the subject. 'So, do you work around here?'

'Yes, I work at a bank in the CBD. And yourself?'

He arched his back on the bench for a good stretch. 'It's

my fourth year of studying Law. Hopefully one day I'll be that reputable lawyer that everyone talks about,' he teased. He had such a good sense of humour–she loved that about him.

'Wow, that's amazing. It requires a lot of hard work and dedication, I admire that,' she said. Then she realised that she was giving him far too many compliments. She didn't want to give him the slightest sign that there was something she liked about him.

'Well thank you,' he said, smiling warmly at her. 'I do love my work–now all I need to do is find the right balance between that and my social life. Once I've mastered that, then I guess the sky's the limit.... By the way, I never did ask you your name,' he continued.

'My name is Angel,' she said timidly.

'That has a lovely ring to it–is it short for Angela?' he asked

'No, it's just Angel–as in an angel in the sky,' she said with a soft laugh. He gazed at her for a while before answering.

'I like that, it's Angelic,' he smiled. Before she could ask any more questions, her bus arrived and she was pleasantly surprised to see him get onto the same bus. It was packed to capacity but he guided her in and made sure she was okay. Then he went over to a man sitting towards the front of the bus and asked him to stand so that the lady could sit. Grinning at her, he pointed to the available seat while he continued to stand next to her.

By that stage, she was blushing so much that she could feel the heat radiating from her face. She was glad he couldn't see her. If this was what love felt like, then.... She hoped it wasn't another dream. She pinched herself and looked up to find him gazing down at her with the cutest smile she had ever seen.

Chapter 10

*S*he awoke the following morning with a song in her voice and a bounce in her step. *Am I falling for Doug or am I just overreacting?* she wondered, afraid that perhaps he behaved that way with all the girls. He had a way with his charm and he did turn many girls' heads.

It was Saturday and this was one of the first that she had chosen not to work. She headed to the shops to buy Katie a gift as she had promised, and looked forward to spending time with her in the afternoon. A panda bear on the top shelf of the toy shop attracted her attention. On its paw were the words 'squeeze my paw'. When she squeezed it, the panda began to talk. 'Hello, what's your name?' it said. When she pressed it again, it asked 'Can you cuddle me?', then 'Will you be my friend?' and 'Can you sing to me?' Angel grinned. This was the perfect gift for a little girl who refused to talk. *Perhaps in time she'll want to answer the panda's questions,* she thought.

On the bus drive to Katie's house, Angel prayed for guidance. It was never easy trying to find the right things to say to her. She was a sensitive and traumatised child, and Angel just wanted to bring her comfort. On arriving, Angel looked up to the sky. A storm was imminent. A fine haze seemed to hang over the house, dulling the sky to a murky grey colour. As she rang the door bell, she could hear Katie's hurried footsteps as if she had been waiting. The door swung open and Katie's warm happy smile was enough sign for Angel to know that this would be a good visit.

'Hello precious girl, may I have a hug?' asked Angel as Katie threw her arms around her. They sat together in Katie's room while Faith made them something to snack on. 'I have a surprise for you. Do you remember that I promised you one?' Angel passed the gift onto Katie. Like any child, Katie ripped the paper off and with wide eyes, she held the panda to her heart. She was even more intrigued and excited when she discovered that it could talk. 'Katie, one day, you will be able to speak back and answer the questions that your panda is asking you,' said Angel gently. She did not want to put pressure on the little girl but she also wanted to give her a sense of hope.

It was a great afternoon and Angel didn't want to leave– but she needed to head back home before the storm broke. Fortunately she did not live too far. She got home just before the clouds burst open. Then the phone rang and it was Crystal. Angel could hear she had been crying again. *Oh no, another argument with Colin,* she knew.

'Angel, I had nobody else to phone, not many people know that Colin hurts me,' Crystal said in a strained voice. 'I may not be able to come to work on Monday, depending how long it takes for the swelling of my bruise to go down,' she said with no further explanation.

Angel felt a mixture of anger and sadness overwhelm her. She shook her head in wonder that Crystal could have so little confidence in herself. She did not know how to get across to her that Colin didn't deserve her; she'd told her time and time again. 'Crys, until you decide to leave Colin, you will never escape the power he has over you...' she began.

'But Angel, he didn't mean to hurt me; he just can't control his temper and he has apologised,' Crystal countered, desperately trying to convince Angel and herself that he was not to blame.

'I won't always be around to help you, and one day he might just kill you,' she retorted, tired of Colin's sugar-coated bullying. That upset Crystal even more and she hung up in tears. *Oh Lord, please open her eyes to the truth, Angel prayed. Make it easy for her to walk away. Help Colin too to identify his weakness.*

Once more Angel could not fall asleep that night. She tossed and turned and eventually threw her pillow across the room in frustration. *Oh Gran, I so wish you were here. I need your advice and your love. It's your turn to be my Angel now and to guide me along.* Suddenly she felt a warm, solid presence. It was precisely what she needed. With a smile she lay on the couch and recalled the good memories.

Turning on the television, her interest was captured by a local programme featuring three women who had volunteered to have a make-over. They were average-looking women when they walked in, and their transformation was nothing short of incredible. Then it struck her how similar last night's dream had been. Hadn't she herself been transformed into a beautiful queen of elegance?

Angel sat up and wondered what this all meant. Was this a sign? Was she meant to do this? Twice in a row seemed too significant for her to ignore. If this was what she needed to do, then she would obey and do as God said. Her leave was due in three weeks and this would be her perfect opportunity to become a new Angel. Perhaps later she would find the reason for it... but she trusted God's plan in her life and was excited to become the girl she had always dreamt of–one who was both loved and admired.

Chapter 11

*M*onday morning could not come quickly enough for Angel. She rushed over to the Manager's office to hand in her leave form. 'Aha...' said her boss as he looked at her leave request. 'I'm glad you've finally come to your senses. We all need a break in life and I trust you'll appreciate some time to yourself.' With that, he stamped her form and handed it back to her.

She was now counting the days to becoming the woman she had seen in her dream. That afternoon she phoned the Agency that had done the make-overs on the programme she had watched. 'Please could you tell me a little more about it–how much it will cost and how long the procedure will take in general?' Angel enquired as she scribbled down all the info she could get.

'The cost depends on what you want done, or what extremes you want to go to,' the lady explained. 'It varies for everyone; but if you are wanting a full transformation which involves a change of hairstyle and colour, manicures, makeup artistry, a beautician, a wardrobe designer–'

'I want it all!' shrieked Angel, unable to contain her excitement any longer. 'I don't want to look like myself at all–in fact no-one must recognise me,' she added, determined to give this her best shot.

She was quoted a price which at first took her breath away. But she had saved up all her hard-earned money for some pleasure too, and she felt she deserved to have some fun. It would only be a once-off treat. Three weeks' accommodation at a Bed & Breakfast was an added option, and she took that too. It would be the holiday and treat of a lifetime. It would take her two full days to be converted into a woman of substance. She had it all planned in her mind and this would be her secret only; no-one needed to know. She would simply tell everyone that she was going away on a three-week holiday.

Back home, she lay in her bath full of bubbles surrounded by lit candles. She allowed her mind to drift. *This is a good thing,* she told herself. Even while other thoughts crowded in, tightening her stomach with doubt, she repeated the words to convince herself. *This IS a good thing.*

When she got out of the bath, she quickly changed and got ready to go shopping. It was pay day and her cupboards were bare. She arrived at the bus stop, still deep in thought, when suddenly she felt a pair of hands cover her eyes. 'Three guesses' she heard a man say and immediately she knew it was Doug. Why hadn't she realised the possibility of seeing him?

'Hi Doug,' she said, surprised at how shy she suddenly became. 'I see you still have no car...?' Words couldn't come– at least not any that made sense to her.

'Yeah, they're really dragging their heels–I'm getting quite fed up with the bus now,' he said casually. 'So, where are you heading at this time of the afternoon?'

'I'm going shopping. A girl's got to do what a girl's got to do,' she laughed.

'Oh, that means trouble,' he teased.

'And where are you off to if I may ask?' she asked inquisitively.

'I have a case study I need to do so I'm meeting up with a

mate from my group at the library,' he explained.

With a sense of envy, Angel nodded and wished him luck. On the bus drive, he sat next to her. Just feeling his arm brushing against hers was enough to bring the colour to her cheeks. *Why do I blush so much around him?* she wondered. It was not like her to blush easily. They got off at the first stop and he turned to wave her goodbye. There was something about him that made him special, yet she couldn't quite put her finger on it.

After two hours of shopping, she gathered all her groceries together and headed for the bus stop. Once again in deep thought, she could feel sleep was slowly catching up on her. The bus slowed down as the robots turned red and Angel stared out of the window. She could see the library and wondered if Doug was still there. Then like a mischievous child, she suddenly had an urge to see for herself.

She got off the bus opposite the varsity and made her way towards the main library. Her heavy packets didn't help, but she finally arrived at the big double doors. As she was about to step in, she heard a crowd of people laughing out loud just a few metres behind the library. Then she saw him amongst four other guys. She ducked behind a bin out of sheer embarrassment, cringing at the thought of appearing to be spying on him. Luckily he hadn't seen her–but what she saw of him was a sight she would not soon forget. He was so drunk that he could hardly stand. One of his mates helped him to the bus stop bench, then left him to find his own way home.

The confusion of what she really felt was driving her crazy. She didn't know if she wanted to hug him or strangle him, maybe both. For a long moment, she stood breathing in slowly and reasoning with herself. Then she fled, not looking back.

Chapter 12

Crystal stared into Angel's face as she told her about the previous afternoon and how Doug had supposedly gone to the library for his case study.

'I told you about his boozing escapades, Angel. Besides who cares, it's not like he's your boyfriend,' she said, waiting for Angel to nod in agreement. Angel knew more than she wanted to know about his reputation but had been determined not to judge him on gossip. Now an instant blush crept into her cheeks. 'No way girl, are you falling for this guy?' asked an astonished Crystal.

'Hey, I did not say that, YOU did!' Angel blurted out, wondering how to change the subject. The more Crystal enquired, the more Angel denied.

For the rest of the day, Angel felt gloomy. Nothing had ever got in the way of her work before, but that day she could not concentrate and made silly mistakes. That soon-to-be holiday was going to be a lifesaver. Knocking off early that afternoon, Angel dragged her heels to the bus stop. She wondered if Doug had his car back from the panel beaters. Either way, she forced herself not to care and tried to convince herself that she didn't need someone like that in her life. Her days of smelling beer breath and listening to slurred speech were over. As she was about to shake herself out of her thoughts, there he was walking towards her carrying his files and books.

'Hey Angelic girl, how was your day?' he asked as he

came over to sit beside her.

'My day was wonderful, thank you.' She wanted to put him on the spot. 'So how did the case study go yesterday?' she asked with her heart pounding in her throat.

'It went well. I didn't finish though; I intend doing that tonight. It never works when you have your mates with you,' he said, gritting his teeth. He clearly had no intention of explaining.

'Yes, I agree. I'll remember that when my days of studying begin,' she said, looking the opposite way.

'You intend studying? May I ask what?' he asked curiously.

'Psychology. I want to be the person that people can come and speak openly to. I want to help families that cannot cope, especially innocent children,' she replied with a choked voice. He nodded and changed the subject very quickly. She knew she had hit a nerve for Doug and wished she knew the story behind his drinking.

When she reached her destination and moved to get up with her heavy bag, he pulled her arm down again. She was mortified. The mere fact that he had made physical contact with her took her completely by surprise. As she looked down at him, he whispered, 'Would you like to go out for dinner tomorrow night?' His big brown eyes glowed beneath eyelashes that most girls would dream of.

She was not sure if she had heard right and nearly asked him to repeat himself. Instead she blurted out, 'Yes, dinner sounds great,' eyes wide in astonishment.

'I'm getting my car back tomorrow so I will pick you up at six thirty,' he said winking at her. She gave him a warm smile as she walked away. In a moment she completely forgot the previous night's doings and walked all the way home with a smile.

Her ginger cat sat on the windowsill waiting for her to come home. 'Mimi, I'm home,' she said as she unlocked the door. Mimi came running along and gave her a welcome rub against her legs. 'Guess what Mimi… I have a date tomorrow night, can you believe that?' she asked. *How could anyone want to have a date with me,* she thought.

Instantly she could hear her Gran's voice saying to her, *Angel, I am watching you and I am hearing you too. Remember what I told you, your beauty within is shining through.* She did not want to start thinking about her gran now; it would make her teary and all she wanted to do was celebrate.

The high pitched ring of the phone broke the silence. She only ever received calls from two people: Aunt Cecilia checking up on her or Crystal needing some encouragement. This time it was Crystal.

'Hey, why don't you and I go out tomorrow night? Maybe we can catch a movie or grab a bite?' Crystal asked for the first time ever. There was no mistaking the excitement in her tone. She had only ever invited Angel to the canteen on Fridays–never a real night out as best friends do. Angel's heart sank with disappointment at having to turn her down. Crystal could sense her hesitation and Angel didn't want her to know about the date–not yet.

'I'm so sorry Crys, tomorrow night is virtually impossible for me but any other night I'm all yours if you're not too upset with me,' she said, dreading being cross-questioned. It wasn't as if she could make up any old excuse because she never had commitments other than feeding her cat. Luckily Crystal didn't ask; nor did she sound too disheartened.

Lying in her bed that night, Angel was thankful not only that she had a date with a gorgeous guy, but she also had a best friend. It had been a good day for Angel and her heart was warm. She could sense that better days were to come and she felt like a child again. Thinking of little Katie, she wondered if she was fast asleep with her panda tucked in beside her.

Chapter 13

*A*ngel kept looking at her watch the next day. She needed to rush off early from work to get herself ready– and that could take a very long time. She knew from experience that it would take her several minutes just to convince herself that she wasn't as dull and boring as she saw herself. This time it would be a consolation knowing that she would soon be transformed into the woman of her dreams.

The sun was setting as she hurriedly walked down her busy road. A car's engine was revving, some teenagers were kicking a ball, and music was blaring from another car whose speakers were about to blow. Seeing her skip her way to the door was an unusual sight for the neighbours who had never seen her so happy before, let alone skipping with joy.

Doug had indeed got his car back that day and was thrilled to be mobile again. Angel was on time and waiting for him in the lounge when he pulled up outside. 'Gran I'm going on a date tonight... someone thought I was special enough,' Angel squealed out loud as she went to open the door.

'Hello,' said Doug, smiling broadly at her. 'Sorry I am five minutes late, to be exact,' he added with a glance at his watch. With a million dollar smile, she locked the house and walked ahead of him to his car. 'Busy road you have here,' he said as he buckled himself in his seat.

'Never a dull moment,' she replied, feeling somewhat

embarrassed. 'I'm glad to see you have your wheels back,' she said, turning the conversation back to him. Luckily he turned on soft music that made her relax a little. In fact something about the way he looked at her made her feel safe and at ease.

During dinner he did not overcrowd her but rather complimented her on everything from her work, to her courage, to her gentle nature. And she knew they were not pick-up lines either; they were real. Doug told her that he had been born in Cape Town but raised in Canada, and had only recently come back home. Her past was not something she was keen to talk about. However they did chat a little about their childhood when they got on the subject of schooling.

'I had a scooter that I dragged all over with me,' he reminisced. 'Bikes were not my favourite, but I think I have my Dad to thank for that.' He paused for a moment. 'My Dad rode over my bike with his car and he never bought me another one after that. If he had ridden over the scooter, I think it would have shattered me to pieces,' he said, chuckling to himself. Angel loved to hear his stories.

'You must have been devastated about your bike,' she sympathised. 'How did he manage to drive over it?' She knew she had put her foot in it when his expression suddenly changed.

'My dad had a few too many drinks that day so–'

'But it wasn't your scooter, so that was the main thing,' she interjected, feeling guilty for having asked. He loved how good she made him feel. There was never an awkward moment with Angel around.

The magical evening went by perfectly until he'd had one too many glasses of wine and his speech began to slur. Moments like this made her want to throw up. She had so hoped to stir his hardened heart and make him repent of his wild ways. 'I think it's time to head back home, I have work in the morning,' she said as she excused herself from the table. He agreed and quickly gulped down his last drink. She was not happy getting into the car with him but her silent prayers protected her like they had in the past.

On arriving back home, he got out of the car and went over to her side to open her door. It was such a pity about the drinking because if it weren't for that, she could honestly say he was the closest thing to perfect. He was good looking, intelligent, well mannered, friendly and a real gentleman too. She did not want him to stick around and see how close to tears she was, so she quickly thanked him and walked away. 'I love your dress by the way,' he called after her before tripping over the pavement.

Walking into her lonely little domain, Angel threw herself onto the couch and sobbed. This was very unusual for Mimi to see. Angel was not the type to cry unless she was devastated. She hugged her cat and told her that life was cruel and she was tired of being unlucky. Taking out her Bible, she looked up one of Jo's favourite verses from Proverbs: *'Who but God goes up to Heaven and comes back down? Who holds the wind in his fists? Who wraps up the oceans in his cloak? Who has created the whole wide world? What is his name—and his son's name? Tell me if you know. Every word of God proves true. He is a shield to all who come to him for protection.'*

Silence was golden the following day at work. Crystal's mood matched hers. She had been crying and her eyes were puffy and red. Angel didn't ask questions. Instead she tried to distract Crystal and make her laugh, even though laughing was also the last thing on her mind. She always put herself last and that was one of her qualities that shone the most.

That evening Angel decided to pay Katie a surprise visit. Faith hadn't been feeling too well so Angel told her to take the evening off and get some rest. She was thrilled at the thought of entertaining her little friend all evening. Katie was beaming with joy when Angel arrived; there was something about her that put Katie immediately at ease. Faith had told her that she reacted differently to Angel than anyone else. Angel had been pleased to hear it, and enjoyed the excuse to lavish Katie with some special fun.

By the time they were done, Angel didn't have the heart to wake Faith up and ask her to take her home. She stayed on a little longer and hoped that Faith would waken and offer her a lift. It wasn't until 8pm that Faith woke up with a jolt. 'Oh Angel, pardon me, I took some flu tablets and they knocked me out–I'm so sorry,' she apologised. She was interrupted by Katie tugging at her mother's nightgown with a note in her hand. It read 'pleez can Anjil sleep over tonite mommy'. So that's how she communicated with her mother, Angel realised. Faith read the note, smiled and handed it over to Angel. 'You are most welcome to stay if you'd like to – I can take you home early tomorrow,' she said smiling.

Luckily it was a Friday night. It took only one look in Katie's direction for Angel to nod and say, 'Okay, I will stay over.'

Katie wrapped her little arms around Angel. She was a very petite seven-year-old with dainty features. Shooing her to her room, Angel cuddled up next to her and read her a story. Before it ended, she had already fallen asleep with the panda snug next to her. Angel started to fantasise again, imagining herself one day lying next to her own little boy or girl. How magical it would feel to hold a child so close to her heart. She instantly shelved that fantasy for another day in the far future, though a part of her hoped the fantasy would soon come to life.

Chapter 14

The next morning Katie woke Angel up with a big hug and a few bounces. Before she knew it, she was being pulled out of bed by the hand–there was no time to lose. Katie didn't want to waste a single minute of her big-sister-friend's visit. Faith made them breakfast before she broke the news to Katie that Angel needed to go back home. Looking at Angel with her puppy dog eyes, Katie pulled a pout to show she was sad. Angel promised to visit one more time before she went off on her three-week holiday.

Angel was a little embarrassed when Faith drove into the neighbourhood but she tried not to allow her insecurities to show. She gave Katie a hug goodbye and watched the car drive off. As it drove away she saw another familiar car driving towards her home… it was Doug! *No,* she shrieked inwardly, *he cannot see me like this. I haven't brushed my hair or even my teeth, and I'm still in yesterday's clothes!*

She pretended not to have seen him and darted into the house, heading straight for the bathroom. She calculated it would take her four minutes–enough time for him to drive in, lock up and walk over to her front door. She swopped her shirt for a clean one, brushed her teeth and hair and still had time to spray before he knocked. Her heart was galloping as she opened the door. 'Doug, wow, what a surprise, please come in,' she said, showing him in. She hoped she hadn't left the lounge in a mess.

'Thanks Angel. I'm sorry for just arriving, but I never did get your number and I wanted to know if you'd like to join me for a picnic today... if you have no plans,' he asked expectantly. She could have sworn she detected a hint of nervousness in the way he stood there with his hands jammed deeply into his pockets. Her own heart was still pounding far too many beats per second.

'Yes I would love to... I've got no plans. Could you give me a few minutes to get ready?' she asked bashfully.

'No problem Madam, I shall wait for thee,' he said, winking at her. One day that wink would melt her into a blob on the ground, she knew it. Angel's head kept saying, *Angel let him go,* but her heart shouted, *No I cannot let him go.* She hurried off upstairs and fumbled over everything. She couldn't find her right shoe. Then she remembered that her lipstick (the only makeup she ever wore) was in her bag which was still lying downstairs on the couch. *Breathe, Angel. You can do this.*

Coming down the stairs she could see him stroking Mimi, but Mimi wasn't impressed with this strange man and wasn't making herself too friendly. They drove off together and chatted about music and who their favourite artists were. On arriving at their picnic spot, she saw that he had packed a woven mat to lie on, a bottle of wine with two glasses, some chips, chocolates and various other snacks.

They started by taking a long walk together, and ended up climbing rocks and even playing hide and seek. Then they lay down exhausted on the mat, looking up at the flawless blue sky. Two families were picnicking a few metres away and between them they counted seven children. Noticing a little boy sitting alone, she remembered the parties she had attended all alone.

'Penny for your thoughts,' said Doug looking down at her. She smiled as she told him how she could recall going to parties and being rejected because she had never fitted the others' income bracket. Then she started to tell him the story of the little boy who had been so friendly and how she had watched him ride his scooter. Then she stopped suddenly, as if a ten pound hammer had hit her.

'Oh my goodness, no it cannot be… no, surely that was….' She couldn't compose herself and he couldn't understand what she was trying to say. He caught the hint of speculation in her eyes. 'Doug…' she began, 'was your scooter red?'

'Yes, how did you know?' he replied quizzically. She looked at him with tears flooding her eyes and she prayed they wouldn't run down her cheek.

'And would you perhaps remember asking a timid little girl to ride your scooter with you?' He cocked his head in deep thought. She could see he was battling to recall, so she asked another question. 'You complimented that same timid little girl and told her that her dress was pretty.' Then the penny dropped, and he squinted across at her.

'Aha, that was Alexis's birthday party, wasn't it? Are you trying to tell me that you were the timid little girl?' he asked incredulously.

'That was me Doug! You made such an impact on me that day that I could never ever forget it. No-one had ever given me a compliment like that–.' She broke down and wept, overcome by the memories and the emotion of finding the same little boy sitting beside her, holding her tight and consoling her.

They held each other for a long time without speaking, and neither one felt awkward. It had been a wonderful day and Angel didn't want it to end. As if he'd read her thoughts, he lifted her chin so that her gaze was upon him. 'Thank you timid little girl for an amazing day,' he said gently. 'May I have the honour of taking you on many more dates to come?'

Her eyes were suddenly as sparkling and bright as jewels. 'Nothing would make me happier, friendly boy,' she said. She blocked out the voice in her head telling her that she was getting too close to this man who had the same disease as her mom.

Together they packed the basket and walked off hand in hand to the car. Her world had come alive and it felt so right. Arriving at the car, he turned to her and slowly bent down to give her a kiss. But she stopped him. As awfully impossible as it felt, she needed to set the record straight and tell him about the screaming voice inside that was warning her about him. Her mouth went dry as she looked directly into his eyes.

'Doug, I know this may offend you and it's the last thing I want to do... but I care too much about you, about us, to let this go unquestioned.' She saw the puzzled look on his face and wished she could just wipe it off and wave her magic wand. Where were her fairy godmothers when she desperately needed to be rescued?

'Go ahead Angel, you can talk to me,' he said as he gently moved her hair from her eyes.

'I don't approve of your drinking, Doug, and I know that there is something deep within you that is driving you to drink. Alcohol is your comfort. I can see that–'

And then the ten pound hammer came crashing down on her again. Flashbacks of Doug's drunken father came to her mind's eye. She remembered how it had hurt her watching him drag his son around like a dirty rag. She stared at him, totally speechless. 'Your father was an alcoholic, wasn't he?' she asked as tears welled up again.

Looking the opposite way, he simply said, 'I think I should take you home now.' She wanted to slap herself in shame, but the voice inside her head reassured her that she had done the right thing. They drove home in silence; she didn't know what to say to him. It had been easier when they were simply friends, when they were only two people searching for answers. Now just being in his presence ignited fires deep inside her, fires she'd never known even existed.

Chapter 15

Two days passed without a word from Doug. She had not felt this sick in her stomach since her beloved granny died. Her heart was at war with her mind. *Oh Lord, where do I go from here? We were obviously meant to find each other, so how can I possibly let him go now?*

Crystal noticed that Angel wasn't herself. 'Hey you, what's up? I can honestly say I've never seen you like this. It's your twenty-first birthday in a few days' time and you have made no plans whatsoever! That is downright ridiculous and I won't have it!' she said, filled with determination to change her friend's mindset.

They went out for a walk after work and Crystal tried to lift her spirits. But Angel was beyond cheering. She excused herself and walked to the bus stop where she sat down to wait for her usual bus. She stared into the sky above as if to find the answers written in the clouds. Instead, the answer came from behind her.

'Would you like a ride on my scooter, little girl?' Those words were like music to her ears, oxygen to her lungs and laughter to her pain. She jumped up from the bench and fell into his arms. They hugged for what seemed like an eternity. She felt relieved of her guilt but it didn't change the dilemma in which she found herself.

'I'm so sorry Doug, I never meant to hurt you. I didn't get the chance to tell you at the picnic that my mom was just like your dad and I know how helpless you felt as a child. I just want you to know that I care and I know your pain.' She stroked his face and cupped his cheek.

'You had no-one to rescue you Doug, I had my gran. God took me beneath His mighty wing and provided for me through her kindness and love. But who did you have, Doug?'

'I'm sorry, I had no idea about your mother... does she still drink today?' he asked innocently. She looked at him with eyes that told a sad tale.

'No, she isn't drinking anymore because there are no alcoholics in heaven,' she replied. He closed his eyes tight and pulled her against him. They had a mutual understanding. They got onto the bus hand in hand and she felt normal, just like the other girls who were happy and in love. God had stripped her bare and now He was rebuilding her house on a firm foundation. Then it suddenly occurred to her that he was catching the bus too. 'And where is your car? Having a rest today?' she asked jokingly.

Alas, it was no joke. There had been another accident the same night of the picnic. He had had one too many beers again and hit a lamppost. There was minimal damage but his car still needed a new radiator. This time she closed her eyes tightly, knowing what the answer would be and not wanting to hear. He opened his mouth to say something but Angel raised her hand to stop the flow of excuses. 'Doug, I cannot fall in love with you in the fear of losing you,' she said.

He put his finger on her lips as if to say 'say no more'. Then he promised her that he would stop drinking because he had missed her so much in the past two days. He had realised that she was a lot more important, he said. The stubborn look in his eyes and the way his jaw clenched made her consider his request.

'I like that.... If I can have your word, I will give you my

70

heart,' she said. He pulled her to him and kissed her. *Wow, so that's what a kiss feels like! No wonder people do that everywhere and anywhere,* she thought to herself.

Her leave was coming up in five days and now she was no longer looking forward to it. But she had made a promise to God that she would go ahead with the transformation; she knew it had been a sign and she was going to wait on His plan.

The next day Doug told Angel that he wouldn't see her because he needed to study for a major exam. She bought him chocolates and a good luck card and, though he was tempted to ask her to join him to share his chocolates, he was very serious about his studies. Angel prayed for him the next day and spent the evening with Crystal for that long-awaited movie and dinner date. They were like two children and giggled their way through the evening. Colin was still giving her a hard time but Crystal kept falling in his trap. Angel could not wait for her to come to her senses.

The next day she waited impatiently for the phone to ring. Doug had promised her that he would let her know how the exam had gone. She had a strange feeling in the pit of her stomach. She worked half-heartedly and on leaving that afternoon, her sixth sense told her to check the pub where he regularly met up with his friends.

The bus driver took his jolly time that day and the longer he took, the more apprehensive she grew. Something wasn't right; it wasn't like Doug to forget to phone. Finally, Angel hurried towards the pub but her legs suddenly felt like lead as she approached it. From inside came the muffled sounds of laughter and the clink of glassware. She hardly had the strength to open the door.

A fire crackled in the fireplace on the far end of the room. At the bar, two men hunched over mugs of beer. They looked up as she stepped in, then just as quickly stared down at their glasses. She searched the room with her eyes. On her right she saw a couple staring intently into each other's eyes. Next to them, a dishevelled old man was swilling a glass of whisky. And there, in the dimly lit corner, she could see Doug sitting all alone. As he turned his head, his eyes widened in astonishment. She walked over to him but her legs felt like jelly.

'What are you doing here?' asked Doug, searching her eyes. He didn't think any woman would come to his rescue, and certainly not Angel.

'Call it morbid curiosity Doug,' she said, choking back the sob. He tried to reach out to her but she turned and walked out. She remembered his promise that he had sealed with a kiss. So it was nothing more than empty words... just like her mom.

She ran to the bus, trying to clear her mind of the memories of their beautiful day together. Arriving home, she broke down once again. She was not sure how many more disappointments she could face. *You have a choice Angel. Choose life or death.* Death would be her staying home tonight and crying herself to sleep; life would be to leave the house and be in good company instead. The only person that she knew would warm her broken heart was little Katie.

She wiped her tears, took a shower and headed for the door before she could change her mind. At the last moment she grabbed a change of clothes and her toothbrush–just in case. It was still light enough for her to run to the bus stop.

At Katie's she instantly felt renewed. As much as Angel always lifted Katie's spirits, the little girl did the same for Angel. They spent a delightful evening together, then Angel read Katie a story in bed. She lay still until she heard the sound of Katie's deepened breathing, then she slowly eased out of bed and joined Faith in the lounge.

Faith took one look at Angel and said, 'What's worrying you tonight Angel? You're not your usual self, I can tell.' Her words were enough to open the floodgates for Angel. Once she had composed herself enough to speak, Angel told her every single detail of her life. The weight of bottled up emotions on her shoulders slowly eased off. This was the first time she felt that she could share her sorrows and burdens with someone she could really trust. Faith was wise and had good Christian values, and they spoke until way after midnight. Faith's advice was to not give up on Doug yet.

'There is a reason why God made you find each other again after all these years,' she said with conviction. 'He has a plan for the two of you, I'm sure of it. Give Doug more time. He obviously has great difficulty giving up this bad habit, but something, someday will click and it will be good enough reason for him to stop once and for all.' Angel felt so much better listening to Faith's advice.

'You have already been through so much in your life, Angel. This is just another one of those trials and I know you'll also triumph over this one. Tomorrow, go and ask Doug exactly what drove him to the pub that night. He might have given in to peer pressure, but maybe something else happened after the exam. Usually it's a weakness of some kind that drives people to drink. Did you ask him?'

Angel shrugged her shoulders. 'He tried to tell me something but I walked away,' she said tearfully.

'There's nothing wrong with that; he needs to see that you are serious and that you are not happy with his drinking. But now that a day has gone by, give him a chance to explain.' Angel hugged Faith and thanked her from the bottom of her heart. 'Angel, I'm just as thankful to you for bringing such joy into my Katie's life,' she said, her voice quivering. She missed her husband and she missed the conversations with her little girl... it was a year in her life that she would never have back.

'She will speak again Faith, I know it, and I know that God has a plan for her too,' said Angel as she hugged Faith goodnight. She climbed back into bed next to Katie and felt the much needed warmth slowly mend her broken heart. She rejoiced over the blessings that God had poured on her. *So why this unending sorrow? How could I ask for more?* she thought as she drifted off to sleep.

Chapter 16

The next morning Faith drove Angel to work. Crystal was in high spirits and promptly reminded Angel that it was her birthday the next day. 'What's wrong with you girl, where's your excitement? You don't turn twenty-one every day you know!' Crystal teased.

'Oh I know Crys, I don't need reminding. And in two days I'm off on holiday too,' she reminded Crystal.

'By the way, where are you going to and how can I contact you?' Crystal asked nervously. She wasn't too keen on the idea of Angel being out of reach for three whole weeks.

'Don't worry about that, I will contact you as I will be going far away,' Angel replied cryptically before walking out the office, leaving Crystal intrigued.

Angel was longing to phone Doug to try to piece together the events that had led him to the bar. Assuming there were any, that is. She wasn't as convinced as Faith. But Faith was right–it was now her turn to contact him.

Sneaking into the boardroom for some privacy, she dialled his number on her phone. With jangling nerves and a sudden rush of blood to her head, she obeyed her heart and waited for him to pick up the phone. There was no reply. *He's probably still in lectures,* said the angel on her shoulder. *NO! He's in the bar and you are being deceived,* shouted Satan. She walked back into her office with her head hanging low. Even with all she had to do, Angel felt a vague disquiet, an aching of loneliness.

'There you are!' Crystal shouted from across the room. 'Now listen to me: tomorrow night you are meeting me at my house and from there, you and I are going out to celebrate your twenty-first!' Crystal squealed as she linked arms with Angel.

'Helloooo, anyone there? Are you smoking something girl?' she chided, seeing the blank expression on Angel's face.

Angel broke into a grin. 'You are the funniest you know that! And I am so glad to have you in my life. Yes, Your Honour, it's a date at your place. My gran would turn in her grave if I were to spend my birthday alone.'

'That's more like it. Now, what do you want for your birthday?' Crystal asked, reaching for her notepad. Angel shrugged, embarrassed. 'Oh no, I can just see I won't get a reply for this either. So it will have to be a surprise then!' she babbled as she went to pour herself another cup of coffee. If ever one looked in Crystal's direction, she'd always have a cup of coffee in her hand.

That afternoon Angel rushed over to the bus stop, not quite knowing if she would see him. He wouldn't have got his car back so quickly, she figured. When her bus arrived, she shook her head and waved it on. She would catch the next bus. This time she did not read her book. Instead, she kept turning around thinking he would creep up on her with one of his humorous chirps. She missed those chirps so much. Her heart ached and her stomach churned.

Go home Angel, a voice said inside. But it was a softly spoken, gentle voice from within; it had to be Jesus or Gran or their angels. At their command, she stood up and signalled the next bus. *He may just surprise me with a visit tonight,* she thought as she stared out of the window at the passing cars.

He didn't, and she went to bed early. As exhausted as

76

she was, she couldn't prevent all her doubts and insecurities invading her mind again. *Stop*, she willed herself and spoke out loud to God. *Thank you Lord, I want to kiss this day goodbye and will look forward to my new blessings tomorrow. After all it is my birthday and I know that I am loved by You. When I have no-one and my world seems dark and empty, I know that You walk beside me.*

The phone rang at 6am the next morning, hauling Angel out of her somnolent state. Thinking it was the alarm clock, she fumbled for it through half-closed eyes until she recognised the sound of the house phone. Running her fingers through her hair, she straightened her wrinkled pyjamas, kicked the rug out of the way and dashed to pick up the receiver. Who could be phoning her at this hour on a Saturday? She would tell them exactly what she thought of them in a moment. 'Hello…' she said softly, so as not to wake herself up completely.

'Happy Birthday Honey!' yelled Crystal so loudly that now there was no questioning if she were awake or not.

'Thank you Crys, but I will never forgive you for waking me up,' Angel teased a little sheepishly. At that same moment, Mimi came crawling along, stretching her body into a perfect arch. Looking up at Angel, she made a perfect leap into her arms. That was Mimi's way of saying 'Happy Birthday'. Angel hung up after twenty minutes and carried Mimi back to the lounge where they cuddled up together for another two hours.

She was awoken by the thudding knock on her door. *Doug*, she thought, *it's Doug, and I am in my pyjamas.* She peeped behind the curtain to look for his car but instead saw Faith's. She ran to the door and within seconds of opening it, Katie's arms were wrapped around Angel's legs. She had drawn her a pretty birthday card with red hearts sprinkled with glitter. Faith had baked her a chocolate cake with a large edible silver key on it.

'Thank you Katie, you have just made my birthday so special, do you know that?' said Angel as she knelt down to her level. She looked up at Faith and thanked her for the surprise visit, at the same time apologising for still being in her pyjamas. She felt so at ease with Faith after their chat. After excusing herself to get dressed, she made tea and they sat outside enjoying the chocolate cake while Katie pampered Mimi with a back rub.

'Well Angel, we hope you have a great day,' Faith added, moving to get up. 'We're off now to do some shopping but we'd like you to walk us to the car.' Katie looked up at her mom and gave her a wink, like a sign of some kind. Faith looked back and smiled and nodded. Angel knew they were up to something. Katie got into the car and pulled out a tiny box wrapped in pretty pink paper and handed it over to Angel. Bursting with excitement, she opened her gift to find a shiny key inside.

Puzzled, she looked at Faith. 'A key..?' she asked.

'Look down the road Angel. What do you see parked under the tree?' Faith asked, looking as if she were going to burst with excitement. Angel's heart felt as if it was going to jump out at any moment. Standing back with her eyes wide in fascination, she took in everything that was happening around her. She couldn't miss it. There under the tree was the most beautiful red lady's scooter she had ever laid eyes on–with a sassy red helmet hanging on the handlebars. She dropped the box in total awe and almost lost her balance.

'No you didn't... no, oh Faith... you didn't have to....' With tears of appreciation running down her cheeks, she reached out to Faith and held her tightly like her precious gran.

'Now you no longer need to catch a bus. And better still,

now it's your turn to ask Doug to share your scooter with him....' she said, winking mischievously.

Angel's happy tears knew no end. Everyone in the neighbourhood came crowding around them, even the pranksters. One guy covered in tattoos started rapping to the 'Happy Birthday' song and everyone joined in. It was a sight to behold–there she was standing in the middle of her road with a congregation of rough-looking rappers closely admiring her new red scooter. It was a moment she would never forget as long as she lived.

It had not even reached midday and her day so far had been flawless. Not quite perfect yet because Doug hadn't phoned or visited. But she loved her precious gift and was grateful for the distraction. After her friends had left, she made an excuse that she needed to go to the shops and zoomed off on her scooter, feeling a rush of euphoria. She loved the way her hair blew in the wind. She felt as if she were flying, and she knew God had given her wings in more ways than one.

That evening, as she was about to leave home, Crystal phoned. 'Hey gorgeous, I forgot to mention that you have to dress for the President tonight. I'm taking you to a fancy place,' she said mysteriously. Angel promptly did as she was told.

Crystal's house was in darkness when she arrived, yet there were so many cars on her property that Angel wondered if perhaps they were guests of her parents. She found a safe spot to park her scooter, grabbed her helmet and picked her way across the dimly-lit garden to the front door. Suddenly the lights flashed on and everyone shouted 'SURPRISE!' Angel squealed in shock. She saw that Crystal had invited everyone from work and their families, and a good number of her friends too. Angel stood back and eyed each person one at a time–some of whom she had never met before. Then, right at the back of the room, her eye stopped.

His presence caught her completely off guard. He walked over and pulled her towards him. His hold made her lose all sense of where she was and her arms found their way around him. Her world stopped for a moment in time and she savoured it like it was her last day on earth. 'Happy birthday my Angel,' he said and wiped the tear from her face.

She smiled tremulously. 'I thought you'd never come back, I'm so sorry for what–' she started, but he put his finger on her lips and whisked her outside. They chatted and laughed while she greeted people coming in and out. Then Angel cupped her hands over Doug's eyes, blindfolding him. Guiding him to where she had parked her scooter, she moved her hands away from his face. He looked like an eight-year-old again as he took in the sight. Turning his face to look at her, she asked him in a child-like tone, 'Would you like a ride on my scooter?'

Chapter 17

*T*he evening was as flawless as her entire day had been. Doug spoilt her with gifts ranging from her favourite music to a gorgeous pair of earrings, chocolates and a romantic dinner voucher for two. She was the belle of the ball and it was all thanks to Crystal. She couldn't help hugging her every time she saw her. Now more than ever, Angel was fiercely determined to see her friend happy and wished she knew how to change her mind about Colin.

By ten o'clock, the dance floor was crowded with raucous people, and everyone was having the time of their lives. Tonight she was not going to be Crystal's chaperone and she was happy to see that Colin was in a corner chatting to other girls. *You deserve to be in a corner, you don't deserve someone like Crystal,* she murmured beneath her breath. Scanning the room, she looked for Doug who had been at her side the entire evening. Then she saw him—pouring a double vodka and coke. If there had ever been a time where she felt her heart bleed, it was there and then.

'*I told you so,*' squealed Satan in delight.

'***Wait on me Beloved, I have a plan,***' said the other voice that could belong to none other than the Almighty. She turned and walked away. Where was Faith now that she needed to ask her what to do next? Sensing the answer, she dismissed her dark thoughts and joined a group of girls dancing.

By eleven o'clock, Doug had become loud and had

knocked over glasses on two occasions. With obvious reluctance, Angel stooped down and started to pick up the broken glass. Despite her good intentions, Crystal didn't make matters any easier when she marched over to where Doug was standing and confronted him. 'I cannot believe that you would choose Angel's special night to screw things up again. Can't you see you are embarrassing her!' she roared with her hands on her hips.

Angel tried to pull Crystal back but Doug retorted sneeringly, 'I wouldn't talk if I were you, look at your life, it's just as messed up.' With that he slammed his fist on the table and stormed out. The angry flush in Angel's cheeks merely added colour to her pale skin. *How did Doug know about Crystal?* she wondered. Looking at Crystal, she saw how she glared angrily back at Angel.

'No... no... Crys, I didn't say a word to him, I would never betray you,' she blurted out, realising what her friend was thinking.

Refusing to discuss it further in front of an audience, Crystal ran upstairs in tears. Angel heard Doug turning on his ignition and revving loudly. She ran after him in sheer panic. 'No Doug, WAIT... please don't go!' she screamed at the top of her voice. The emotions together with the cold night air caused Angel's throat to ache, so much so that she hardly had a voice. She opened the car door of the passenger side and got in. 'Angel, please get out of my car.' He looked exceedingly angry. 'I've disappointed you one too many times... I don't deserve you.' His voice dropped to a whisper but Angel did not move.

'I'm not leaving Doug, I will not allow you to drive anywhere. Give me the keys,' she said firmly, holding her hand out to him. 'Please Doug, hand over the keys,' she pleaded, her panic rising. But in a blind rage, he sent the car in reverse.

It thudded into the car behind. He then shifted to first, jammed the wheel to the right and floored the accelerator. They jerked forward and the car swerved wildly, throwing Angel against the door. Squeezing her eyes shut, she braced herself... but the crash never came. He simply stopped; and she wasn't sure if it was because he had damaged his car for the umpteenth time, or something else.

She turned to him with an expression of abject despair. 'We've run out of options Doug. Look at it as a nice way of saying "we've reached the end." She did not want to be alone, but how much more could she count on Doug? She stopped reproaching him, satisfied with his stunned look. He heard the desperation in her voice and reached his hand out to touch her–but she pushed him away and got out of the car.

Wild and reckless with fear, she ran. She struggled against panic and the premonition that she would lose him too, just like her mom. All her senses became raw. 'Angel, wait... come back,' he shouted after her, but she kept running and didn't stop. She didn't take all the usual precautions she'd learnt to take during her teen years; tonight in her confused state, it was irrelevant. Pausing to lean against a lamp post until her breathing slowed, she realised that the street light was a beacon that made her look vulnerable standing beneath it. *Time to move Angel,* she thought and turned around.

She could see Crystal's house in the distance. The cars were leaving one at a time. Dragging her heavy legs to where her scooter was parked, she was unsure whether to leave there and then, or try to console Crystal and patch things up with her. *But my heart is just as torn,* she thought. As always, her compassionate side got the upper hand and Angel walked into the house. Crystal was sitting on the floor with her knees tucked up into her arms. 'What an Oscar-winning performance Angel,' said Crystal sarcastically.

'Crys, I've never betrayed you–' Angel began.

'Just leave Angel,' Crystal spat back. 'I'm so confused right now, I don't know what to believe anymore.'

Angel knew it wouldn't help trying to convince her when she was in this kind of mood. 'Thank you for the best birthday I have ever had, Crys. I will never forget today and I am sorry that one person had to spoil it for us. He will never do that again,' she said as she walked out into the night. She moved mechanically towards her scooter and allowed the tears to flow freely in the wind as she drove away. Her wings had been broken, but she would wait for them to mend again. Her holiday would be the first step.

Chapter 18

*S*unday morning dawned bright and full, the sky a beautiful blue. The smell of roses outside her window wafted through the bedroom. Her first thoughts were of Doug and she tried to shake away the memories of the previous night's episode. Despite what she'd said to him, she couldn't bear the thought of not seeing him for the next few weeks. *God please take away the empty longing in my heart. I don't want to NEED Doug anymore, I just want my soul filled with thoughts of YOU.*

Angel stretched her body across the bed and on seeing the time, she jumped to her feet and headed for the shower. Today was the last day she would look like Angel. Excitement started to rise in her throat in anticipation. She packed her bags, then ran next door to her neighbour who had promised to feed Mimi for her in her absence. Then, leaving a window open for Mimi, she stroked her one last time and said out loud so Jo could hear, *I am going on holiday Gran. And although I may look like Cinderella, I will still be the Angel you know. I would appreciate your checking on me from time to time. I know there is a reason for this, Gran, but I will find out in time–God's time.*

Then she turned around and walked out. The bus stop felt far out of reach as she dragged her luggage behind her. Her first stop would be Katie's; she could never leave without saying goodbye. She would spend every waking moment with that little girl if she could. Luckily their home was just two kilometres away. Approaching it, she could see Katie playing outside with her puppy. Then, as if she knew Angel was watching, she looked up and ran over to the fence, waving profusely.

'Hello gorgeous girl, may I come in?' Angel yelled, and within a few seconds, she had opened the gate.

Faith was always happy to see Angel. 'And where might you be going with that big suitcase?' she asked, giving Angel a big hug.

'I'll be away on holiday for three weeks and I've come to say goodbye to you and Katie before I leave,' Angel said softly. Then, knowing she needed someone at home to confide in, she briefed Faith on her real plans. Taken aback at first, Faith soon agreed that she needed to follow the leading in her heart.

Taking Katie for a walk in her big garden, Angel gently told her she was going away for a few weeks. The little girl held onto Angel's hand and it was obvious that she was gloomy; but she perked up when Angel made her promise to draw her some pretty pictures in her absence. After an hour of visiting and as many cuddles as she could give, Angel stood up and lifted Katie in her arms. She kissed her on the cheek and reassured her that she would be back soon. Then Faith drove her to the bus stop and watched her board the bus, as a typical mom would. She waved them both goodbye as the bus drove away. They were like family to her and she had no doubt that she would miss them plenty.

An hour later she arrived at her bed and breakfast. She was welcomed by the owner, Mrs Smith, who showed her around and took her to her room. 'Dinner is served at 5.30pm every evening and breakfast tomorrow is at 8am. As explained over the phone, I don't cater for lunch but there is a great salad bar across the road if you like," she rattled off. 'Not that you can afford to eat salads, my dear. I will need to fatten you up a little,' she added with a chuckle.

Angel liked her already. 'Thank you, I won't miss your meals and look forward to some home cooking,' she replied warmly, rubbing her tummy. 'Oh and Mrs Smith, I must remind you that I won't be here tomorrow night and the next.'

At first the older lady looked questioningly at Angel, then she remembered their telephone call. 'Yes of course, you will be sleeping out for two nights whilst finalising your make-over. I hope to recognise you when you get back,' she teased.

'Well my plan is to be unrecognisable, so we'll see about that!' laughed Angel. 'Not that I'm a fugitive of any kind," she giggled. 'It's just a personal accomplishment, if you know what I mean.'

Mrs Smith smiled knowingly. 'Well, have fun and enjoy the pampering and if you change your mind in the night, I'll be happy to take your place tomorrow,' she said with a wink as she left the room.

Angel's room was beautifully decorated in soft pink and lilac. Her bed was a king-size one with lilac lamp shades that gave off a soft light on either side. The large plasma screen mounted on the wall in front of her made her feel like a queen. What more could she possibly ask for? Her tummy growled as she looked at the clock. In a few minutes she would make her way to the little dining area.

After combing her hair, brushing her teeth and touching up her pale pink lipstick, she walked over to the other side of the big guest house. She could see that Mrs Smith had green fingers. Her garden was well maintained, the grass was a lush green and there was no denying that it got watered daily. Although it was still early evening, the path was attractively lit with twinkling lanterns that made the garden look like a picture from a fairytale book.

On entering the dining room, she counted six elegantly laid tables. She chose the one closest to the window, where she could see the sun setting over the mountain. On her left was a lively family of five and behind her in the corner was a man in his late thirties who sat alone. He hardly acknowledged her as she walked past to get to her table. Two single people eating alone seemed so unnecessary, but she far preferred it that way.

The meal tasted delicious: roast chicken, mashed potatoes, green beans and gravy, salad and rolls. Since she hated to cook for herself, she often grabbed take-outs or pre-prepared meals. But she longed for more frequent home-cooked cooked meals and hoped she would acquire some kitchen skills before marrying one day. If she ever did.

Once again thoughts of Doug crept into her mind. *Stop it!* she yelled at herself, sorrow seeping from her heart like the tears brimming in her eyelids. In its usual fashion, her gut clenched and she struggled to finish her food. On returning to her room, Angel collapsed onto her oversized bed and heaved a mountainous sigh. She leaned into her suitcase and pulled out her Bible, guiltily wiping off a fine layer of dust. It fell open to Isaiah 41. Verse 10 and 11 almost leapt off the page at her. *'Don't be afraid, for I am with you,'* it read. *'Don't be discouraged, for I am your God. I will strengthen you and help you. I will hold you up with my victorious right hand. See, all your angry enemies lie there, confused and humiliated. Anyone who opposes you will die and come to nothing.'*

Oh Lord, she prayed. *Tomorrow I begin the journey that You have set out for me. It feels right and justified, which can only mean that it comes from You. Please help me to learn what You want me to. And may this experience touch the lives of many in ways that I cannot begin to imagine, but You know.*

When her eyes grew heavy, her mind wondered over to Doug and this time she allowed her thoughts to take on their own paths. The mere sound of his name incited bittersweet memories and a stirring of guilt mixed with longing... a longing she could not put into words but which wove itself into a beautiful dream she never wanted to end.

Chapter 19

The high-pitched sound of the bedside alarm woke Angel with a jolt. The day had finally come when she would walk into her make-believe world. Her emotions were one big knot and the butterflies in her tummy were at war. The wholesome breakfast prepared for her did little to settle her nerves.

'So you didn't change your mind after all, that's too bad,' teased Mrs Smith as she cleared away Angel's plate.

'Thank you for the lovely breakfast Mrs Smith. My nerves are a little wobbly, hence the leftovers on my plate,' Angel replied awkwardly.

'Don't be nervous; look at it as a once-in-a-lifetime opportunity. If you don't like your new look, you can always go back to who you were–and I assure you there's nothing wrong with Angel,' she said encouragingly. Angel blushed at the compliment and thanked Mrs Smith before leaving.

It was a ten minute drive on the bus and Angel could not sit still. She was convinced that the lady sitting alongside her could hear the pumping of her heart. At this point in time Doug was the last thought on Angel's mind. She kept checking her watch, afraid of being late for her first rendezvous at the salon, but thankfully she was running on schedule.

The make-over salon was an attractive three-storey building set in a small garden edged with elegant topiary trees. She arrived on time for her first hair appointment which was on the second floor. As the elevator door opened, she stepped into the hallway and felt her body tingle with nervousness. The salon was busy with women–some under dryers, some at the basins, some with foils and others with curlers. She reported at the front desk and before she had a chance to announce who she was, her name was called and she was led to the back of the salon.

'Hello, my name's Sam,' said a nattily dressed young man, holding out his hand.

'Pleased to meet you, I am Angel,' she replied, shaking his hand and looking about, unsure what came next.

'I believe you have requested a change of colour and style?' Sam asked, looking down at his book.

'Yes that's right and I would love to hear your suggestions,' Angel replied, hoping she appeared more confident than she felt. Sam sat her down, then looked at her face and her limp blonde hair.

'Hmmm… my thoughts would be either red at shoulder length as it is, or short and dark–perhaps even black and styled like Cleopatra, or –'

'Yes, before I change my mind, I'll settle for the short, dark bob,' Angel said. Cleopatra sounded very exciting.

Lifting and fluffing her hair one way then another, Sam analysed her hair carefully and eyed the dead ends. Suddenly he looked doubtful. 'You do realise that your hair is very fine and we would need to cut off quite a bit of dead hair,' he said. Thinking aloud, he continued. 'We may need to make it wispy rather than the straight cut... or... but hey, we are here to make you beautiful, so leave it to us,' he reassured her as her eyes widened in anticipation.

'Oh no, I really liked the sound of a Cleopatra look… but I do understand that one needs thick hair for that kind of style...' she replied, a little disappointed.

Cocking his head with his finger on his lips, he thought for another moment. 'I do also have the most striking wigs which could be another option. I happen to have the perfect one for you if you'd like to give it a try?' He wanted to see her happy and her heart warmed toward him. She was glad that for the first time, someone could start taking care of her hair so that one day she could freely choose the style she wanted.

Minutes later he returned carrying three different wigs. He was right in saying that they looked no different from real hair. She tried on the long brown curls first and they both burst out laughing. Then she tried the long auburn red hair but that was also out. Finally she fitted the short black bob with the straight cut fringe. It was perfect! It was as if it had Angel's name written all over it. They both agreed that her original hair would need a cut and a good treatment, and the wig would fit perfectly over her natural hair. No-one would know the difference. After long thought, she decided on the wig–not that she ever imagined herself wearing one, but it suited her make-over, sealing it to perfection.

She was led to the basin and for the next two hours she was pampered and faffed over like a bride on her wedding day. Through the window, Angel watched a cluster of leaves blowing about in mid-air. The wind had picked up and afternoon was setting in. Having been offered coffee and biscuits, she had enjoyed every minute so far. Having a friend share this experience with her would have been optimal, but looking around she noticed a few women who were alone like her. Her mind drifted off to Crystal, knowing all too well that this pampering was what she would have loved.

She recalled Crystal telling her that she went regularly to the salon for her manicures and back massages. Lost in her thoughts, she was patted on the shoulder and finally told that she could look at herself in the mirror. Her feet felt heavy from the long sitting period as she made her way to the mirror. Her heart skipped a beat and she clapped her hands over her mouth. Her hair followed her jaw line in a striking Chinese bob, and the way it fell made it seem thick and full. Without the scraggly dead ends, it made her face look instantly more alive.

Then it was time to fit the wig. It was thick and shiny black and shaped to perfection. And it fitted like a glove over her own hair, complementing her porcelain doll complexion without making her appear too pale. Her heart skipped a beat at the strong, elegant reflection that stared back at her. 'I don't know what to say, except... I LOVE IT!' she said with tears in her eyes.

She had another half hour to go before her next manicure and pedicure appointment. She was given the key to her room along the top floor of the building, and after unpacking she admired herself in front of the mirror for at least fifteen minutes. Every cent she had spent on this make-over was feeling more and more justified. Again she thought of Doug. Although she shouldn't have expected or even hoped for it, she'd been almost certain that he would have called her by now. But then maybe he'd been waiting for her to make the first move. Locking up, she went back to the floor below and looked for Room 208. As she walked in, the soft background music and the dim light drew her in.

'You must be Angel,' said the voice from behind the curtain. A smart, white-clad African lady by the name of Beauty came out to greet her. She took one look at Angel's bitten nails and told her she had every reason to be here. Long false nails would be quite a challenge for Angel but they settled for that and a French manicure. Beauty was gentle and precise, and Angel's hands looked magazine-perfect when they were finished.

Her feet were another challenge. Beauty guessed correctly that she did a lot of walking, and she gently massaged the tension out of her feet before attending to their grooming. When she was done, Angel was literally walking on air–never before had her feet felt so young and full of bounce. Looking down at her beautiful hands, she pictured her grandmother's diamond ring on her second finger. ***One day Angel. Be still and know that I am God. I have a plan.***

'I know Lord,' she whispered. She had woken up that morning as the dull Angel with the adolescent pony tail and nonexistent finger nails. Now a pretty brunette with long, elegant nails stood in her place. She was slowly becoming the princess of her dreams. She smiled and looked up at the sky through her bedroom window. Even the stars were calling her name.

Suddenly she had an idea: she would change her name too–just for now. She would be Angel back home, but she needed to be someone else first. A few names crossed her mind but none sounded classy enough. Cindy Crawford was her favourite actress but Cindy didn't work for her, even though it could be short for Cinderella. She remembered how Granny Jo had always called her the 'belle of the ball' whenever she went to a party. *Belle… it means 'beautiful' in French,* she realised, smiling. *Yes!* she yelled, skipping her way around her room. *My name is Belle.*

It had been a good day and she couldn't wait to see what tomorrow would bring. She knew that Belle would turn many heads. In spite of herself, Angel laughed–something she'd rarely done since she last saw Doug.

Chapter 20

After a big breakfast the next morning, Angel tried to get comfortable on her bed. Her first appointment of the day was only at eleven o'clock, so she flipped on the television. It had been a long time since she had watched weekday television, and she settled on a Mr Bean movie.

Halfway through, she decided to go for a walk. The sun looked so inviting, spilling golden rays on the rooftops. Relishing the warm sun on her shoulders, she leaned into her bag to answer her vibrating cell phone. It was Doug. Her knees felt weak, as if they were barely able to hold the weight that had just piled onto her shoulders. Choosing not to reply, she hoped he would leave her a voice message. Alas not. No sooner had he hung up the phone than he tried again. Tears burned her eyes as she forced herself not to answer. Remembering their last incident, she resolutely zipped her phone back in her handbag and carried on walking.

Shortly before eleven she presented herself at Room 204. She was greeted by big mirrors and row upon row of clothes on rails. Every variety possible was hanging before her, from evening wear to daywear and beachwear. On the opposite end were rows of shoes: flat ones, heels, boots and sandals to suit any culture and all types of feet. Her look of admiration was like that of a child walking into a room filled with dolls of every kind.

'Okay, let me see, you must be Angel,' said a tall, slim

lady in stiletto heels. *Why would an already tall woman wear heels to make her look abnormally tall?* Angel wondered curiously. *Perhaps she would soon find that out.*

'Yes, that is my name and I am astounded at what I see,' said Angel with a sparkle in her eyes.

'That's great! I'm Elize,' said the tall lady, sizing Angel up through her sophisticated glasses. 'I will start off by explaining each dress code and what styles would best suit your body shape. Then we'll move onto the shoes and match them to the correct gear.'

They walked up and down the racks of clothing, with Elize explaining that clothes with lines running vertically would be beneficial for her petite frame. Angel listened attentively, taking note of what to wear and what not to.

'When it comes to footwear, you should consider wearing heels to enhance your height – even small ones,' Elize advised. For Angel it was like being given a ticket to the world of grown-ups, let alone permission to make the most of her assets in flattering clothes and high heels. She could barely contain her excitement at the thought of the shopping spree waiting for her. This time she knew exactly what to buy.

When her hour session was complete, and after trying on at least twenty different styles of clothes, she mustered the courage to ask Elize one question. 'May I ask why you are wearing heels, being as tall and elegant as you are?' she asked, feeling herself blushing.

'Very good question, Angel. It shows that you have been listening and learning. There is only one reason–and it is not by preference, I assure you. It is my job to look glamorous, so tall or not, I have to wear the heels.'

'Well glamorous you are, and thanks so much Elize. I will carry this with me my whole life long,' said Angel as she turned and walked out. She could not contain her excitement; this was every girl's dream. Looking at her watch, she wondered if she had time to head for the mall. Her next appointment was only in two hours. The closest mall was a few blocks away–too close to catch a bus but too far to walk and still get back on time. She decided to hold onto that idea till after her next session. In that way, she would not be rushed and could shop to her heart's content.

Angel went back to her room and stared at her cell phone, tempted to phone both Doug and Crys. Oh how she missed them both already. It felt like a part of her was left behind. Then she looked through her photos and on seeing Faith, she decided to phone her and ask how Katie was doing.

'Hello Angel, so good to hear your voice. How is your holiday so far?' Faith asked excitedly.

'It's been amazing so far Faith, but my heart goes out to Doug and I miss him terribly. I wish I knew what to do, but I'm waiting on God to show me,' said Angel, sighing heavily.

'That's right Angel, ask God to guide you. If Doug is meant for you, then you will be together when the time is right.' Faith's words of wisdom and optimism were precisely what Angel needed. She was so grateful to Aunt Cecilia for inviting her to her Christmas Eve dinner. If it weren't for her, she would never have met Faith and Katie. She couldn't imagine life without them.

Angel wedged the pillow under her head and made herself comfortable. All the excitement of the last two days had exhausted her, and she drifted off to sleep. It was by sheer luck that her phone rang just before her next appointment, waking her up with a fright. It was an unknown number and by the time she reached it, it had rung off. *Lord, was this YOUR doing so that I wouldn't miss my appointment? Why do I even ask... I should be declaring, 'Lord, thank you for my wake-up call, I know it came from You'.*

She rushed down to Room 201, which happened to be the furthest away. Opening the door breathlessly, she stepped into a multicoloured land of lipsticks and nail polish. It was a beautifully decorated room with rows of dressing tables equipped with all kinds of makeup. The posters on the walls were of smart women of all races, each beautifully groomed. Each and every one of the sessions so far had had Angel's mouth gaping open in admiration. *I don't know how much more excitement I can take!* she laughed to herself.

'Are you ready for your transformation?' a man's voice said as he came towards her to shake her hand. 'Hi, my name is Roger,' he said, showing off two beautiful dimples as he smiled.

'Hi, I'm Angel' was all that she could say. She was quite taken back at his gentle eyes and soft-spoken manner. Her first impression of him was that she could speak openly to him without feeling too intimidated. Seating her in front of him, he gazed into her face and once again, she felt the rush of blood heading straight to her cheeks.

'So I see we have some instant blush,' he chuckled, making her cheeks feel even hotter. She felt at ease with him as he continued reassuring her that she needn't be shy or afraid. 'Why is it that so many women are afraid to wear makeup?' he asked, noticing Angel's bare skin. 'Once we are done, you will never want to go without again,' he said with a conspiratorial wink.

Roger taught her how to apply makeup to each part of her face. He suggested the colours that would match her skin tone and which colours would suit her hazel eyes. She was very nervous when he worked around her eyes. It tickled her and they kept watering until eventually he sat back and laughed. 'You remind me of Baby in *Dirty Dancing* when he needed to teach her the dance and she would laugh when he touched under her arm,' he laughed.

Remembering the part he meant, she started to laugh too. He made her feel so at ease that their one-hour session became almost two. He took his time, making sure that by the time she left, she was able to apply her own makeup with confidence. Looking at his watch, he realised he was running late. 'We have come to the end of our session. I hope you enjoyed it and that I haven't scared you for life,' he teased.

'No, quite the contrary,' she replied. 'I feel like a woman now and not a young girl anymore, thanks to you. I used to love watching my mom apply her makeup when I was a little girl but –'

Roger heard the choke in her voice. 'Well now you can go and show her that her little girl has grown up,' he said, oblivious to her sad story.

She got up to leave but a huge crocodile tear out of nowhere ran down her cheek, leaving a long black streak in its trail. Suddenly she was self-conscious. This was not the time, she thought. True to her first impression of him, Roger grabbed a tissue and wiped away both tear and mascara trail.

'Thank you so much Roger for this experience of a life-time,' she repeated, then turned to go.

Chapter 21

*B*ack at her room, she found an envelope under her door. It was addressed to 'The New You'. She opened the envelope to find a note which read:

Dear Angel

My staff and I would like to thank you for your patronage and hope that you have thoroughly enjoyed your stay. To thank you for purchasing this package, we have added a final mystery session to conclude your treat with us. Kindly proceed to Room 202 at 2pm before checking out. We truly hope this has been a memorable journey and look forward to seeing you again.

Yours in grooming
Ben Grant
Director

Another session! squealed Angel in sheer delight. Due to her last extended session, she didn't have much time to pack and still eat lunch. She rushed over to her room and packed her bags, thinking she'd grab a quick cup of coffee in the canteen on the way to Room 202. Luckily the canteen was not busy. As she turned with her hot coffee in hand, she bumped into Roger.

'Aha, I see the makeup is still intact, so I didn't scare you too much after all,' he said with the same warm smile.

'Not at all,' she smiled back. 'And this time you can't see me blush as it is well camouflaged by the professional himself.'

'Can I join you for coffee?' he asked and she nodded eagerly in response.

'I only have twenty minutes before my mystery session but I would love you to join me.'

He pulled out a chair for her. 'Mmmm, I know all about this mystery session and I am sure you will savour the moment,' he smiled enigmatically.

'So, have you been working here for a long time?' she asked as she stirred the sugar into her coffee.

'Ten years now. I've been a makeup artist for movies too. And the awful accident scenes you see on the television with scarred faces and oozing blood... that's what I do as well. It's not only about a pretty face.' She gazed at him intrigued. 'I've worked with certain famous actors and actresses too,' he said in a matter-of-fact manner. They chatted for a few minutes, taking intermittent slurps of coffee.

'Well, I had better leave you now to head off to your surprise session. It was great meeting you. And if ever you decide that grooming is not for you, I can assure you that the natural look was just as attractive,' he said.

Angel's heart warmed to overflowing at his generous compliment. 'Thank you so much Roger. It's good to know that I may be noticed one day–with or without the paintwork.'

She waved him goodbye as she rushed off to the very final session of her wonderful, fairytale stay. On arriving, she found herself amongst ten other women sitting in a row. Each one of them had 'curiosity' written on their foreheads. She grabbed her chair and then the lights went dim and a DVD was shown. The Director himself appeared on the screen.

Welcome ladies. By now you will have gained much knowledge on how you can improve your look using the simple tools we've shown you. As a token of our appreciation, we are offering you a free eyebrow tint and wax, a spray tan, a make-up application by our makeup artists, and lastly a back massage. This should see you off on your way. We hope you will enjoy the pampering and enjoy 'THE NEW YOU'.

The silence was broken by all the ladies jumping up, clapping and shrieking in excitement. They were then led by their own consultants who transformed each woman into a beautiful swan. No-one was permitted to look in the mirrors until the 'final reveal'. Angel's heart raced and her hands were wet with perspiration – this was her moment. After what seemed like an eternity, her consultant turned to her and led her to a full length mirror. 'Voilà,' she said beaming.

Angel closed her eyes until she was directly in line with the mirror. Then she slowly opened them. Before her stood someone she had never seen before. Her black hair shone in the light, her makeup was flawless, her lips were kissable, her eyes danced and her cheeks were alive with glow. Putting her hands to her mouth, her perfectly shaped white nails added class to her picture-perfect appearance. Turning to her consultant, she thanked her profusely.

'You are welcome Angel'.

'No, my name is Belle,' she replied.

Chapter 22

The next bus back to Mrs Smith's B&B was the last for the day. It would depart in ninety minutes. Angel could not waste time just sitting around. Feeling so beautiful, she wanted to flaunt it and smile confidently at the world. If ever there were a shopping moment, it was then! She had never been a fan of crowds or malls, so shopping–especially alone–ranked low on her list of favourite things to do.

Today was different. Wearing jeans that accentuated her perfect curves, Angel walked from shop to shop with a permanent grin. She was amazed at how much more people noticed her now that she was attractive. Even the sales ladies in boutiques came to her assistance at the bat of an eyelid.

'We have a sixty percent discount on all eye-shadows and lipsticks today,' said a lady looking straight at Angel. It was a good opportunity to see if she gave her the same colour advice as Roger. They chatted for a while and indeed, she knew her stuff. It was that day that Angel bought her first set of makeup.

From there, she moved onto shoes and then onto clothes. While waiting her turn in the fitting room queue, she recognised a lady who had attended the same make-over programme. Their gazes met as Angel walked towards her. 'Hi, it's good to see a familiar face,' she said with a smile that beamed confidence. 'My name is Belle.'

'Hi, mine's Kerry. I see you're also shopping alone,' said the middle-aged woman.

'Yes I'm doing a last bit of buying before my bus leaves in an hour. If you're not in a hurry, perhaps you can help me decide on some shoes?' Kerry nodded and they both agreed that women cannot shop for shoes alone. They spoke about the programme and the competent consultants and beauticians and Angel was surprised when Kerry revealed her age.

'They did a great job with this old woman that I am... I mean... was.'

Angel looked questioningly at Kerry. 'If you don't mind me asking... how old is "old"? Because you don't look a day older than thirty-five,' said Angel.

'Well... you've made my day, my darling. You can add twenty years to that,' said Kerry, hugging herself in joy.

Angel's mouth dropped open. 'Fifty-five? No way!' Kerry was beautifully groomed and had the figure of a teenager, not to mention the witty personality.

'Trust me, before my make-over I did look my age,' she teased as Angel shook her head in disbelief. They chatted non-stop on the way back from the mall and parted ways as Angel boarded the bus. She was still thinking of Kerry and how well she carried herself when her phone vibrated. It was a message from Crystal. Angel couldn't retrieve the text fast enough.

'Hi Angel, I miss you. It's not the same without you. Please give me a call and I'm sorry, sorry for everything,' it read. Relief washed over Angel. She had missed her friend and wondered why she hadn't called 'til now. She immediately replied to her message with 'I miss you loads too Crys. I will make contact with you shortly.'

She stared out of the window, thinking back to the night of her birthday. It had been the happiest and most miserable day of her life. How could Doug have known about Crystal and Colin? Crystal had been so secretive about her bruises. The bus slowed down as it reached the robot and Angel could see her mother's old house to the left. It had been more of a commune for her and her friends. The garden had never been taken care of, and she remembered how she had played alone in the tall grass, chasing the dogs. It was in even worse repair now, with overgrown bushes, weedy flowers and waist-length grass.

Angel purposely turned her head the other way and waited for the bus to move on. For the rest of the journey she allowed her thoughts to wonder about Doug and what he was doing while she was away. *How will I survive two more weeks not seeing him?* she wondered. *Then again, maybe he was having the time of his life at the varsity parties.* The bus finally arrived at her stop and she hurried towards Mrs Smith's guest house, dreaming of the lovely dinner awaiting her. A man cycled past her and stared so hard at her that he almost missed the pavement. Angel giggled to herself–for a moment she had forgotten that she was the beautiful Belle.

As she opened the door to the main dining area to look for Mrs Smith, she saw that she was in time for dinner. She didn't realise how hungry she was until she was walking towards the food. Her stomach rumbled and she even felt a little nauseous. Three tables were occupied and everyone looked at her as she walked past. She hid her surprise with a knowing smile. Choosing her usual table in the corner, she noticed that the same guy who had sat alone the first time was now gawking in her direction. She saw a conflicted expression cross his face as she sat down. Then he got up and walked towards Angel, on whom all eyes seemed to be centred.

'Are you going to eat alone?' he asked as she just got comfortable.

'Yes I'm alone–the chair next to me is my Mr Invisible,' she chuckled without looking in his direction.

'Would you mind me filling Mr Invisible's place?'

Looking somewhat disinterested, Angel nodded. She was tired and didn't feel like making conversation. A quiet uneasiness settled between them. He kept staring at her and Angel wasn't too far from being creeped out. She saw a wedding ring on his finger and was immediately enraged. He was definitely smooth talking her into more than a friendly chat.

'So why is a beautiful girl like you sitting alone? Are you on business?' he asked, chewing robustly on his steak.

'You guessed right, I'm here on business and I'm presuming you are too – else your wife would be accompanying you,' said Angel with pink cheeks.

'Yeah, well... I can't always drag her along with me, someone's got to stay home and look after the place,' he said cockily. 'So what do you say after supper, we go and hit the club down the road,' he said, changing the subject. 'I heard it's the place to be.'

She was certain that people could see the steam blowing from her ears and nostrils. What happened to decency? What happened to purity and faithfulness? To her, life was more than pleasure; it was duty and honour, it was building a family. 'I bet your wife is the nicest, sweetest woman, waiting for you to come home,' she said. He kept quiet and she continued more boldly. 'So tell me, do you always chat up the ladies on your business trips?'

This time it was Angel's turn to stare at him. He seemed disturbed, as if this dinner chat was going to send him back for his fourth beer and his eighth cigarette. 'What is your name by the way?' she asked as she held out her hand to shake his.

'Name is Tom,' he said, shaking her hand. She grinned–a

grin that spoke of her confidence that her words had done their job, keeping Tom from saying anything he shouldn't. They chatted a little more and then Tom, realising that he wouldn't get any further with Angel, got up and excused himself.

She smiled at him as he got up to go. 'Nice meeting you Tom. Enjoy the club tonight.'

Angel sat at her table alone until the last group of people left. She was shocked at how easy it was for married men to pick up women, especially the attractive ones. Deep in thought still, she saw Mrs Smith tidying the tables and looking over her shoulder at Angel. 'I'll help you tidy up Mrs Smith,' she said, walking over to where she was standing.

'Angel... is that you?' she asked, taken aback.

Angel smiled. 'It is I,' she said, spinning around like a ballerina.

'My goodness, talk about a transformation!' Mrs Smith replied, clapping her hands. They remained in the dining area for the best part of an hour, enjoying each other's company and making small talk. Suddenly Mrs Smith looked at Angel with a puzzled expression. 'I'd love to know why you decided to transform yourself, Angel... but if you don't want to talk about it, it's fine with me.' Mrs Smith said as she poured herself a cup of hot chocolate.

Angel nodded. 'You may laugh at what I'm about to say but quite honestly, I don't know the reason yet. Let's just say I'm doing what God wants me to do; this voice inside me just says I needed to obey my gut feeling.'

The elderly lady was quiet for a moment before continuing. 'I don't find it bizarre at all Angel. In fact I admire the way you trust your instinct. I truly hope you find the reason. Does it have to do with a man in your life?'

Angel looked down, guessing it would be the next question. 'Not really, it's a personal accomplishment, more than anything. A part of me was tired of feeling lonely and unattractive. I've always wanted to know how it would feel to be looked at and admired.'

Angel was opening up her heart to a perfect stranger, and she felt her cheeks reddening at the thought. Clearly Mrs Smith found it quite natural, for her next question was, 'And what have you learnt from your experience so far?'

'Well quite honestly, I have loved the attention so far but I've also grasped how quickly one can be deceived as a result of one's looks.' Mrs Smith nodded as if to say 'my thoughts exactly'.

'I don't want to put any thoughts in your head but I think if someone were to ask you that same question in months to come, you might just say that you miss the old you,' Mrs Smith said with a warm smile. Angel nodded and thanked her for the open chat.

'See you at breakfast,' Mrs Smith replied, waving Angel goodbye.

'I wouldn't miss your breakfast for the world,' Angel grinned, giving her a hug. That night in front of the television, Angel was tempted to send Doug a message but she needed to be strong. Just a few more days, then she would pluck up the courage to phone him–and hope with all her heart that he would answer.

Chapter 23

$\mathcal{I}$n the days that followed, Angel fell into a routine of sorts. It felt as if day by day, sometimes even moment by moment, she was gaining back a tiny portion of her identity, discovering afresh who she really was. It had been eleven days since she had left. She was craving Crystal's company, not to mention little Katie's.

Winter was on the doorstep and the autumn leaves lay in heaps outside her window at Mrs Smith's. Dressed in her warm fleecy gown, she lay on her bed one evening, staring at the memoire box she had brought with her. She had kept a few items that belonged to Jo, together with envelopes that seemed of importance at the time. Jo's rings were also hidden in the same box. It wasn't the first time she'd gazed at the box these past two weeks. She had not felt prepared to look through it as yet but she decided she could at least open it. She was surprised at how long she had put off carrying out that one simple chore.

She got under her blanket as she heard the sound of the wind outside. The cold crept in beneath the door. She thanked God for the promise of winter after a long, humid summer. Looking into the box, she saw faded letters, school reports, a small trophy and an old book of poems. One envelope was addressed Sally—but it seemed like Granny Jo had never had the heart to give it to her. Angel reluctantly thumbed through the pages and started to read:

Sally my love, as your mother and your friend, please take my advice and spend more time with your daughter. She is of no burden to me but she needs a mother's love. Your friends and social life will one day leave you but your daughter remains forever. Do not be angry with me, I am only doing as a mother should. Even if you were to take my heart and run it through a shredder, my life would still be richer for having loved you.

Angel could not read anymore. At this moment, she thought she might know what her mother had been feeling years ago. Tears rolled down her cheeks as she carefully refolded the paper. She lay on her bed imagining how she would one day hold onto her children and never let them go. Lying face-down in her pillow, she sobbed. The emotions had been bottled up for so long and it was time just to let go. Unswerving in her faith, she got down on her knees. *Oh Lord, I am still waiting on You. Where do I go from here? My heart is in shreds, my mind is in turmoil and I am desperately lonely,* she cried.

The reply came without delay. ***Precious child, trust ME. As long as you give me all of your heart, you can be sure I will keep it safe.*** The inner voice spoke precious truth into her spirit.

I do give You my heart Lord, and I will continue to wait upon You because I know You have a plan for my life... with or without the man I love. Angel fell asleep to the sound of the wind whistling through the trees.

Then a dream came to Angel. Everything was distorted and swirling with mist. She was running through the streets, crying out Doug's name. She heard his footsteps ahead of her but he was out of sight, beyond her reach. Then suddenly the footsteps were behind her. She was no longer the pursuer but the pursued. When he emerged slowly from the mist, there was her safety, her warmth.

She woke up in a sweat and kicked off her blanket. Sitting up with her head in her hands, she re-lived what she had just dreamed. The need to see him was intense. She knew now that she needed to find him–and only then would he find her. She tossed and turned for the rest of the night. Before breakfast she went to look for Mrs Smith. She had been easy to talk to and she felt compelled to ask her what the dream meant.

'Mrs Smith has gone to do her shopping, she is only due back at ten,' said one of the kitchen staff. Subdued, Angel walked over to breakfast. She was the first one there and enjoyed a quiet room all to herself. With not much of an appetite, her stomach was in a knot. Her gut feeling was telling her something but it was unclear. Faith came to mind so she decided to phone her. The phone rang for a long time before Faith answered in a whispery tone.

'Hi Faith, it's Angel. Sorry, did I wake you?' Looking at her watch, Angel realised it was way too early to phone anyone, let alone ask for advice.

'No Angel, I've been awake and I'm just lazing in bed. What's wrong, you seem tense?' Faith let out a huge yawn, or so it sounded. Angel told her about the dream and her longing to see Doug. After a pause, Faith had the perfect suggestion.

'Angel, I think you need to go back and see him. Don't forget, he won't recognise you and you don't need to make yourself seen. But as long as *you* see *him*, it will make it less painful,' she said with assurance in her voice. 'There's no need to reveal to anyone who you are–and don't go back home,' she added. 'Try and find a B&B close to the varsity and continue with your holiday. You will soon know how you really feel when you see him.' Angel was silent. 'You will also judge for yourself how he seems to be managing without you.' The silence continued.

'Angel are you still there?' Faith wondered.

'Yes, yes, I like what I'm hearing Faith,' she said with excitement in her voice.

Faith had one last piece of advice. 'Angel, you must be prepared if it's not what you expect it to be.' Angel nodded to herself. This was the perfect idea and her dream was indication that she needed to find *him*, on *her* terms.

'Oh Faith, I cannot thank you enough. What would I do without you? I will come and visit you when Katie is at school and you can see the new me. You are the only person I've told. I feel I can trust you Faith.'

Angel's chin quivered as she fought back the tears and said goodbye. She raced to the bathroom to do her face. It had been a full week of the morning makeup ritual. It was time-consuming and annoyed her somewhat, but she needed to fit the part. Her nails would soon need a touch-up, both on her hands and feet. She waited in anticipation for Mrs Smith so she could break the news to her that she was leaving. Even if it meant that her money would not be reimbursed, Angel didn't mind. She had enjoyed her stay thoroughly and learnt more than she could possibly have imagined.

She went and sat on the step outside to wait for the red Polo to drive in. Mrs Smith was a widow and Angel admired her for her strength and ability to run such a reputable establishment. When she arrived, Angel offered to carry her bags.

'Angel, what a nice welcome from you, is everything okay?' she asked as she passed the packets onto her.

'Everything is fine Mrs Smith, but I would love to have some coffee with you if you have the time. I need to ask you something,' Angel replied.

The older woman looked at Angel and could tell that it was important. Once the kitchen staff had taken the groceries,

Mrs Smith sat with Angel. She listened attentively while she told her of the dream and of Faith's suggestion. She saw no condemnation in her expression, but rather an awed fascination.

'I cannot tell you what to do, dear child, but I think Faith may have the right idea. There is no harm in going back home to assess the situation. You may get hurt though, so you must guard your heart. It would be best to see for yourself if this relationship is meant to be,' she confirmed. Angel beamed with joy–this was the third sign that she needed to go.

'I will not charge you for the next few days, Darling. Keep your money and go in peace, knowing that I will be thinking of you,' the older lady added maternally. 'By the way, I see a sparkle in your eye... I think this could be love.'

Angel hugged her like she would have hugged Jo and Faith. What more could she ask for than another 'mother' to give her good advice when she needed it. *God is so good.* She packed her bags and went downstairs to say her final goodbyes to Mrs Smith. 'You had better let me know what comes of this,' she said with a giggle. 'I am very curious and just as excited as you are.'

'I will be back Mrs Smith, this is not the last you'll see of me,' said Angel, blowing her a kiss as she walked out the door. She wondered if she would see Doug sitting at the bus stop. Clutching her stomach, she tried to calm the butterflies that flew in by the dozen. This was her moment, but would she be strong enough?

Chapter 24

Stepping off the bus, she took in the sight of her home town stretching into the haze. She breathed deeply and closed her eyes. *This is home.* Stopping over at two B&Bs along the way, she was told that neither had vacancies. In a panic, she wondered where she would go from here. Scanning the adverts outside the municipal library, she found one listed a few blocks away. She found it easily and realised the varsity was within walking distance. Angel knocked at the front door of the quaint, Dutch-styled house.

'Hello, I'm looking for a room to stay for the next few days. Do you have any available?' she enquired. The forty-something man nodded and welcomed her in. The smell of fresh mint tea and freshly baked choc cake whetted her appetite more than she cared to admit.

'Yes, we have a room and you can stay as long as you need to,' he told her. 'My name is Jake by the way,' he said, holding his hand out to her.

Angel felt relieved. 'Hi I'm A... um... my name is Belle,' she stammered, forgetting who she was for a moment.

'We offer breakfast every morning from 8am,' Jake said as he gave her the keys to her room. As she walked off in the direction he'd shown her, he stared at her like she was some kind of movie star.

Her room was small but comfortable. It was fully

carpeted, which was a bonus because the winter chill was creeping in quickly. She unpacked all her belongings and caught a glimpse of herself in the mirror. It was not often that she stood in front of one, and it still startled her to see Belle looking back at her. She was not ready to go back to Angel– she was on a mission and she would do what God had set out for her to do.

Grabbing her boots and thick jacket, Angel went for a walk to the closest shop for a few groceries. The wind blew her hair and she was enjoying the sensation until she remembered her wig. Sam had said that they don't easily come off, but she pulled the hood of her jacket over her hair just in case. She loved the purity of nature and despite the smell of exhaust fumes and trucks, the wind held some of the power that came with that purity.

Finding her way to the store, she walked passed a beauty salon called 'Beauty with Liz'. She took down the number and made a mental note for next time when she needed to touch up on her hands and feet. After grabbing a few items from the store, she headed back home. She was too tired and unprepared today to walk to the varsity. It required her to mentally psych herself up first. Tomorrow will be the day, she thought, hoping with all her might that her fears would be allayed.

She waited at the pedestrian crossing, watching the cars go by. Suddenly she stood in frozen shock as she saw Doug's car approaching. With fright, she instantly dropped her packet, scattering her slabs of chocolates all over the pavement. The very same impulsive passion that had pushed her to seize an opportunity like this could also land her in trouble. Cursing beneath her breath, she bent down to pick them up, very aware that her cheeks were strawberry red.

As she stood up, she saw his car go past with his friend

Craig in the passenger seat. They stopped a few metres further in front of the 'Bread and Bake', the best bakery in town. Varsity students flocked there for their delectable fresh pies, breads, cakes and Chelsea buns, and Angel knew this was her moment to walk across to the same shop. None of this had been rehearsed, and she was certainly unprepared... but it might just be the perfect opportunity after all.

Daylight was half an hour from fading. Watching as they both got out of the car and went into the shop, she quietly followed suit. People were hovering over the fresh rolls and there before her eyes, just a few steps away, was the man of her dreams. For a few seconds that stretched into twenty, she couldn't keep herself from staring. She clamped her mouth shut and wished she had a hidden camera in her coat pocket to catch her own shocked expression. No doubt about it, he had caught her off guard. He looked a whole lot handsomer in his leather jacket and his dark eyes made her dizzy.

As he turned in her direction, her cheeks went a deeper pink than usual and she hoped he wouldn't notice her. Thank goodness for the makeup. Mechanically she packed rolls into her packet, still eyeing him surreptitiously. Then she realised that Craig had seen her staring at Doug, which made her heart pound even more. Sure enough, Craig poked Doug's side and said, 'Hey Dougie, that bird is staring at you.'

Doug shrugged. 'Let her stare,' he said indifferently.

'Perhaps you know her Dude, why don't you look?' Craig insisted.

'I've got nothing to look at,' Doug replied, but glanced in her direction anyway as he picked up a men's magazine. 'No further discussion necessary,' he said as Craig did all the looking for him.

Eyes and mouth wide open, Angel absorbed all of it. She felt oddly abandoned and had no idea what he was insinuating;

she simply longed to run into his arms. *Not now Angel, you have a mission to complete,* she heard the voice in her head say. Obeying, she turned around and walked out of the store. She was tempted to visit Faith and tell her everything, but decided to wait for the next day when Katie was at school.

She briskly walked back to her B&B and locked herself in her room for the rest of the evening. A quick sandwich would suffice for her dinner tonight. She washed all the makeup off her face and lay in bed, eyes staring into space. *What will tomorrow bring?* she wondered before praying with all her might that she had not made a mistake in coming back home.

Chapter 25

*A*ngel woke up to the sound of a lawnmower outside. Looking out her bedroom window, she could see a very pregnant lady mowing the lawn. It was odd enough to see a woman doing this chore, let alone a pregnant one. She dressed quickly, doing her hair and makeup in record time so that she could get to breakfast promptly. She was the first to arrive in the dining room where Jake was reading the newspaper.

'Hello Belle, did you have a good night?' he asked, dropping his newspaper slightly in order to look over it at her.

'Yes thank you,' she said absently, her thoughts still on the pregnant lady. 'Who is that mowing the lawn?' she asked, trying to appear casual.

'That's my wife Dayna. She cannot sit still for a moment and finds things to do all day, regardless of my constant nagging that she ought to sit and relax,' he replied. Angel wondered why Dayna would even think of mowing the lawn in her last trimester.

All through breakfast 'Belle' could feel Jake's eyes sawing through her. She felt awkward and in moments like these she wished she could be Angel again. Finishing up in a hurry, she had one objective and that was to see Faith. As she walked back up the stairs to her room, she had a feeling of destiny and purpose coming through her veins like hot larva. What would today bring? She dialled Faith's number and immediately she replied.

'Hello Angel, so good to hear from you! When are you visiting?'

Angel smiled. 'So you're not just a pretty face but a mind reader too I see,' she teased. 'Would now be appropriate or are you out?'

'Well, I'm on my way to the mall, but perhaps we can have coffee together,' Faith suggested. It was the perfect plan, and Angel told her she would meet her in an hour.

Walking out of the front door, she could see Dayna and Jake sitting on a bench in the garden. Dayna looked uncomfortable and ready to pop, but he didn't seem to be too perturbed by her groans. For a moment she just stared at them, struck by an odd sense of empathy that she couldn't place.

While she was waiting for the bus, two men alongside her were purposely speaking out loud in order for her to hear. 'So here's your chance buddy. You always wanted to marry a beautiful brunette,' said the one to the other. Turning to face her, the other one went down on his knees.

'You remind me of Snow White. I was wondering if you'd like to marry me,' he said with a straight face while his friend laughed out loud.

Turning to face them ever so slowly, she said, 'If I had to take this wig off right now, you would run a mile. Perhaps I should do that so that you can get the message..?' she said seriously, reaching for her hair.

'No, no that's not necessary, I take back my proposal,' her would-be wooer said quickly, getting up and walking off with his friend. Angel listened to the sound of their laughter echoing in the distance as they beat a retreat. *Lord, I no longer like being attractive. How many more days do I have again?* she asked herself, counting them on her fingers.

The mall was busy with Easter approaching. She could

see Faith in the coffee bar and walked up to her, forgetting for a moment that she was Belle. 'Don't I get a hug?' she teased as Faith looked through her towards the door.

'Sorry, do I know you?' she asked. Then Angel remembered–Faith hadn't seen her transformed yet.

'Well, here is a hint–both our names are frequently mentioned in the Bible,' she replied, enjoying the game. Putting her menu down, Faith continued to stare bewildered. Then getting up, she smiled, wild with delight.

'Angel, I cannot believe this!' she wept as they exchanged hugs. Faith was gobsmacked at her transformation. They chatted for almost an hour until they eventually got onto the subject of love. 'I'm glad you saw Doug yesterday, it's a start,' said Faith. It felt good talking to her–especially when she was unsure of her feelings and needing direction.

'How is Katie?' asked Angel, noticing her photo on Faith's phone.

'She misses you immensely. When the doorbell rings, she thinks it's you and races to the door. And every night she draws a picture for you so be prepared to receive a bundle,' Faith replied with a laugh. Angel smiled but felt saddened that she still had a full week left before going back home.

'Please tell her that I will see her soon and that…' Angel paused, surprised by the emotion shortening her breath.

'Don't worry Angel, she will be fine and she knows you're coming back,' reassured Faith. They hugged one another goodbye and Faith watched Angel as she walked away, feeling like she had been touched by an angel. This girl had a rare empathy and strength of character that made her name uncannily appropriate.

Angel's next mission was to see Crystal, even if only from a distance. She was missing her terribly. After long thought, she decided simply to walk into the bank–she knew by now that no-one would recognise her.

It felt like an eternity since she had last gone to work. When she stepped through the glass doors, she felt as nervous as she had on her first day there. The banking was busy and she recognised the faces of the usual clients. Walking to the back, she saw that they had put another lady temporarily at her desk. She could not see Crystal but imagined that she was probably at the coffee machine. Mr Reid was waltzing around the bank as usual, offering assistance. Standing in the queue, she prayed that he would by-pass her. Her looks may be deceiving but her voice would certainly betray her. For a moment she felt panic rise in her throat–she hadn't thought of that. Before she had a chance to find a quick solution, Mr Reid was standing beside her.

'Good afternoon Ma'am, are you needing to make a deposit?' he enquired politely.

Trying to avoid direct eye contact with him, she briefly replied in a French accent that she wanted to make a withdrawal. He thanked her and walked over to the next customer. Her legs felt weak but at the same time she was proud of the way she had reacted. Giggling beneath her breath, she looked casually towards the coffee machine. Lo and behold, Crystal was making what was probably her fifth cup of the day. Angel smiled and longed to run over to her, but restrained herself once again. Stepping out of the queue as if she had just remembered another appointment, she made her way swiftly out of the bank. She had seen her friend and that had been enough to please her.

Seeing two of her favourite people in one morning without their knowledge had been oddly draining. Angel decided to call it a day and go back home. The weather was turning grey and icy cold and the thought of a nice hot bath and a movie in bed sounded appealing.

Dayna was in the dining room when she walked in. 'Hi Belle, grab a cup of hot chocolate, it's really cold out there,' she gestured amiably before sticking out her hand and introducing herself. 'Hi, I'm Dayna. My other half told me about you,' she said with a twinkle in her eye. Angel liked her immediately.

'Good things, I hope!' she smiled back at Dayna, shaking her hand back. She couldn't keep her eyes off the young woman's bulging tummy, which looked in desperate need of support. She paused for a moment, hesitant to ask how far she was into her pregnancy. 'So when is baby due Dayna?'

'Two weeks to go,' she said, blowing a heavy sigh as she rubbed her belly. 'Well, I will have to come back and visit the little Miss or Mister,' Angel replied as she excused herself and went to her room.

Minus shoes and wig, she suddenly felt liberated. Bathing forgotten, she stretched her body across the bed and drifted into a deep sleep. These two days of excitement and emotion had worn her thin. Two hours later, she was awoken by the ringing of her phone. Fumbling for it in her bag, she was elated to see Doug's number show up on the caller ID. Suddenly she was wide awake, her heart jumping with strange little pitter-patters. Then reality struck–she could not reply. *One more day Angel,* she chided herself. *Tomorrow you will see him and judge for yourself.*

She felt awfully guilty, but he needed to see that she was serious about this relationship and that he needed to change his bad habits. When it stopped ringing, the silence of the room cut like a knife. She was about to put the phone down when she saw that he had left a voice message. Breathlessly she retrieved it.

'Angel, it's me Doug. I don't really know what to say except I miss you terribly and I promise to make it worth your while when you return. Take care of yourself,' it read. She stood trembling from head to foot. The room went blurry from her happy tears. *He still cares, he hasn't forgotten me! Gran, Doug loves me!* she said out loud, skipping her way around her room like a child.

Chapter 26

The first thing Angel did the next morning, before even getting out of bed, was retrieve Doug's message again. Just hearing his voice was enough to make her day. Lazing around all morning was part of her plan. It would only be later in the afternoon that she would make her way to the varsity. The birds outside her window flocked together to greet her as she pulled her curtains apart. The winter sun shone through, casting a beam of light across her bed and revealing a thin layer of dust on her bedside table. *Another beautiful day, thank you Lord, it's good to be alive!* She reached up onto her tippy toes and stretched her arms up into the air.

Glancing at the bathroom mirror, she could see a positive change in her natural hair. It looked healthier and bouncier than ever before as it framed her heart-shaped face. Crystal would surely be satisfied now, after months of nagging her to get it trimmed.

Arriving first at breakfast, she was greeted by the smell of percolated coffee and fried bacon. Going over to dish up some porridge, she was greeted by the cook. 'There is no porridge today,' he said apologetically as he added more bread to the toaster. That was odd–Dayna was always up early to make the porridge herself.

'Have you seen Dayna this morning?' she asked him but he shrugged his shoulders, unsure himself. Angel dished up her eggs and bacon and went back to her table. After eating, she waited around in the dining area for Dayna but there was no sign of her or Jake. Other guests were coming in for breakfast and they too were surprised and disappointed when they saw no oats. A businessman was noticeably in a rush and he asked for Dayna.

'I'm not sure where she could be, would you like me to pass a message onto her when I see her?' Angel asked politely.

'Well, I wanted to tell her that she can finalise my bill as I will be leaving in the afternoon. But not to worry, I can catch her later. I have to say though, it's the first time in the two years I've been coming here that I haven't seen her welcoming her guests at the door. I wonder what's up.' He thanked Angel and walked out, lost in thought.

Angel went back to the table and tried to veer her mind in another direction, but thoughts of Dayna immediately surfaced. Guests had come and gone and she was left alone. *Lord, I can't shake this feeling... something tells me she's in trouble. What can I do Lord?*

On impulse she made her way towards Dayna and Jake's room. She felt awkward venturing into that side of the house but she was left with no choice. Walking away and ignoring her gut feeling would be shameful of her. The door was closed so she knocked. No reply. She knocked again, calling Dayna's name, and with each knock she became more convinced that she was in serious trouble. Going outside, she looked through the window but could see nothing through the closed blinds. A surge of adrenaline blasted through her veins but she maintained a calm tone. Running back downstairs, she asked the cook if he might know where Jake had gone.

'Every morning, Mr Jake leaves early. I think he goes to gym and then he gets the groceries,' he told her as he peeled a potato.

'Would you know who has a spare key to their room?' she asked. The cook shook his head.

'But I do have Mr Jake's cell number,' he offered.

'Yes yes, quickly get the number for me please.' She followed him to the back of the kitchen where he gave her both their numbers. First Angel tried Dayna's number but it went to voice mail. Then she dialled Jake's number, praying that he would answer. Relief washed over her when she heard his voice on the other end.

'Jake, its Angel,' she said, but he remained silent. 'Jake, can you hear me?'

'Yes I can, who is Angel?' he asked. Then it dawned on her that he only knew her as Belle. With no time to fret or be embarrassed, she quickly corrected the error.

'Ah, sorry, I mean it's Belle. Angel's my nickname.' She stopped briefly and went on. 'Jake, is Dayna with you? We can't find her here.'

'No, of course she is not with me. She should be buzzing about as usual. Is... is she not?' As the urgency of the situation dawned on her, Angel told Jake to hurry home straight away. 'I will leave now but it will take me twenty minutes or so,' he said.

That was too long but Angel had no choice but to wait around. She searched the big garden, thinking perhaps Dayna had fallen. Then she searched the empty rooms in case she had collapsed while making a bed. She was nowhere to be found. She bit hard on her lower lip, hoping the pain would distract her from this sudden surge of emotions. Walking to the driveway, she sat on a rock and waited for Jake. When his car finally pulled in, she ran over to him. From his expression she could see he wasn't worried in the least.

'I've searched high and low but I think she may be in her room still,' she said, her panic rising. Jake grabbed a set of keys and together they went upstairs. As he unlocked the door, Angel felt a sudden weakness in her knees, afraid of what she would see. Sure enough, there Dayna was–lying unconscious on the floor. Angel stared, round-eyed in terror. There was a step ladder next to her and Angel presumed that she had fallen while trying to reach up high.

Springing into action, Jake immediately phoned the ambulance while Angel took Dayna's hand and prayed. *Lord, I believe You brought me here on time and that You have Your hand upon Dayna and the baby. Please Father God, let it not be too late.* The ambulance was on time and they did a remarkable job. Dayna kept slipping in and out of consciousness and the baby's heartbeat was low. Just hearing that the heart was still beating was a comfort for Angel.

'We need to get her to a hospital immediately,' one paramedic said to her. 'She has already begun with contractions.'

As they wheeled her into the ambulance, Angel gave Jake a little push. 'Go Jake, I don't mind holding the fort for the day.'

Thanking her through a voice now thick with emotion, he jumped into the ambulance beside his wife. Angel felt nauseous from the emotion of the last hour. *Lord, of all the B&Bs, You brought me here to this one because You knew Dayna needed me. You are so gracious Lord and always on time.*

Angel's day dragged by slowly. *Lord, I was not meant to see Doug today. He was not part of Your plan. In the meantime, I continue to wait upon You,* she prayed, knowing God was in control. The afternoon winter sun filtered through the front door and Angel made herself comfortable in the lounge next to the phone. She was engrossed in a magazine when Jake walked through the door. Angel jumped up, not quite knowing how to read the expression on his face. Then he shouted out, 'I'm a Father!'

She had never seen him so full of emotion before. Angel clapped and jumped up in the air. A little sob of relief slipped past her throat, tempting her to give him a big hug–but she held back. She couldn't quite read him and thought it best to maintain her distance. 'Congratulations Jake!' she screamed nevertheless. 'And so… is it a he or a she?'

'It's a girl and we have named her Belle,' Jake said with a proud smile. Angel's jaw dropped wide open and she was hit with a wave of emotion.

'I am so honoured, thank you,' she stammered, hugging Jake in spite of her reservations. He laughed.

'And Dayna is fine. She had to have an emergency caesarean but she insists on seeing you so…'

Angel cut him short. 'Yes I want to see her too... I'll go over there now while it's still light enough.'

She dashed to her room and grabbed her jacket. Waiting at the bus stop, she longed to be back on her scooter again. Excitement bubbled from every part of her body as she made her way to see Baby Belle. She had no doubt that she would be as beautiful as her name.

Chapter 27

Angel stopped at the nursery window to gape in wonder at the many cribs of pink and blue blankets inside. She loved children, and moments like these took her breath away. Clearing her throat, she walked into Dayna's room.

'Belle, you came,' Dayna said weakly, holding her hand out to Angel.

'Congratulations on your baby girl Dayna. I cannot wait to see her,' she said, giving her hand a gentle squeeze.

With tears welling up in her eyes, Dayna thanked Angel with all her heart. 'You saved my life, our lives,' she said as she wiped the tear that trickled down her cheek.

'You are welcome Dayna. If you had not been the busy body that you are, I may have not responded the way I did. It wasn't like you to not be working at that time, and I could sense there was trouble.' Angel took her hand.

'Yes, I have often been asked why I never sit still. But it's me who runs the B&B. Jake attends to the guests but I do the rest to make sure that everything runs smoothly. Jake wouldn't find it important to mow the lawn or to replace the flowers in the vases or fix a creaking door…'

Angel could see she was flustered. 'Well good for you. Your hard work obviously pays off–I see you have regular clients that have been there for years. You must be doing something right,' she reassured her.

Angel finally had Jake figured out. He was as content

as any man could hope to be, living with a woman who did everything for him. They sat for a while, wrapped in their private thoughts. Then Angel excused herself as she needed to catch the bus before it got dark. She went to view the baby through the window before she left. Belle was the daintiest little girl she had ever seen, with delicate features and the tiniest little fingers sticking out of her blanket. Fifteen minutes later, she was still staring. Then she overheard someone behind her mention the time and she raced out before she missed the last bus.

Back at the bus stop, her heart skipped a beat when she saw Craig walking towards the bus. She wondered if Doug was with him, but he was alone. As the bus stopped, he got in and Angel followed. Sitting behind him, she watched as he messaged someone on his phone. Then it rang. She leaned forward in her seat, trying to catch who he was speaking to. She hoped it was Doug but instead she heard the name Colin.

'What's up? Keen to meet for a gaming session tomorrow?' he asked jovially. 'It's just a couple of us, and leave your girlfriend at home–this is guys only.'

He ended the conversation and hung up. Angel wondered if it might be Crystal's Colin. He was also a varsity student, doing his final year in accounting. *No, of course not, don't be silly now Angel,* she said to herself. Then the penny dropped. *If he IS their friend, then that's how Doug got to know about Crystal's abuse.* If ever friendships were tested and forged, it was now. The puzzle pieces were starting to fall into place.

Arriving home, she threw herself on the bed. What a day it had been. The birth of little Belle had filled her with a surreal hope that lingered against all odds. Lifting her wig and roughing her yellow blonde hair, she did not want to care about washing off her make up tonight. She ate a microwave mac and cheese and then curled up on her bed. Tonight was a good night to watch a chick flick, she thought. Halfway through, her eyes became heavy and she slipped into her world of make-believe.

A fierce wind rattled her window the next morning. She had planned to do a lot of walking today so she declared there and then that it would NOT rain. She only had four more days, then it was weekend and time to go back home. Come Monday, she would be back at work and this chapter would be behind her. She prayed fervently that an exciting new one would have opened by then–one she hoped would be called 'happily ever after'.

Jake was in the dining lounge attending to guests. After her breakfast he stopped her as she walked out. 'Belle, Dayna and baby are coming home today,' he said with a grin.

Angel beamed. 'That's wonderful Jake. Belle will bless your lives with happiness and joy that you never knew existed.' She smiled, turned and walked away. She could feel Jake's eyes on her back. He liked her for her wit, her sweet smile, her affection and her contagious enthusiasm. There was something about her.

Angel looked down at her nails, noticing that they were in desperate need of touching up. She phoned the salon that she had recently passed at the mall. 'Hi, my name is Angel. Would it be possible to book a manicure either today or tomorrow?' Liz sounded like a busy lady; she could hear her phone ringing in the background.

'Hi, yes, I can slot you in at two today.' It suited Angel perfectly. Just before leaving that afternoon for her manicure appointment, Angel phoned Faith to check on Katie.

'She asked for you today Angel,' Faith said. 'She wrote me a note asking how many more sleeps were left before seeing you.' It warmed Angel's heart to hear those words.

'Less than a week Faith, and then I'm home for good.

I'm more than ready to come back.' They chatted for a while longer until Angel had to leave for the salon.

It wasn't a long walk but Angel felt somewhat lazy that day so she decided to catch the bus. She sat behind a couple who had clearly just got married. She just knew from the way the girl kept staring at her wedding ring. She watched the two lovebirds as they laughed, cuddled, kissed and talked. A happy marriage in the making, she mused enviously. Staring out of the window, she allowed her usual thoughts of Doug to drift in and out of her mind, along with images of Crys, Katie and Faith. She loved them all equally–well almost–and missed them more than the moon misses the night.

Arriving at the salon, she found that Liz was still busy with a customer. Her phone rang non-stop, and Angel almost felt compelled to answer her calls for her. After the third caller, Liz let the phone ring on. But this person was persistent and kept trying. Finally she excused herself in exasperation. 'Hello? Oh it's you Crystal. No I haven't forgotten. What time do the banks close on Saturday? I could fit you in then.'

Angel could not believe her ears. *Lord, You really are taking me places! What is it that You want me to do for Crystal?* She couldn't stop a lopsided grin from escaping. Liz then called her in and she thoroughly enjoyed her pampering. She was easy to chat to and Angel could see why she was so popular. She recalled Crystal telling her that if her beautician were to move, she would move too. *Lord why did You bring me to Crystal's salon, of all salons? What do You need from me? Just give me a sign Lord.*

'Thank you Liz,' she said when she was finished. 'I will be needing to see you again sometime soon for my pedicure but there is no urgency,' said Angel as she put her wallet back into her bag.

'I can see you on Saturday if you wish....' Angel stared at

her zombie-like. 'For the pedicure that is,' Liz added, noticing the strange look on her face.

Lord, that is the same day that Crys will be here. 'Ah... yes thank you, that would be wonderful. What time would suit you?' Angel asked, trying to look meek and sincere.

'How about twelve noon? It will be the last appointment of the day.'

Angel confirmed the time and thanked Liz for fitting her in. Walking out, she looked up at the clouds scudding across the sky. *Lord, if You need me to be there on that day, I will be. It has all been so coincidental that it can only be coming from You. One day, I will know the reason for it all.* Looking at her watch, she saw she had enough time to get to the varsity and still wait around for Doug to finish lectures. Her heart leaped at the mere thought of seeing him again.

Arriving at the parking grounds, she casually strolled around until she found his car. It had a surf sticker on the back window and a huge dent in the bull bar which he had not repaired after his last accident. Even if it meant standing at the car all day, she would do it just to get a glimpse of him again. She rested her back against his car door and waited. Then in the distance, she could see the students all leaving the building, dispersing in separate directions. Walking away, she stood around pretending to wait for someone. She watched the students, some walking in clumps and others alone, but Doug was nowhere to be seen. She wondered if he was staying on at the library. Waiting a little longer she saw Craig walking out with a girl. He was walking in her direction and caught a glimpse of her. She casually turned her head, pretending to look elsewhere. They parted ways and the girl walked to her car alongside Doug's. Without any thought about the ramifications, she walked over to her.

'Excuse me, would you perhaps know Douglas Stevens

and where I might find him?'

The girl smiled at Angel. 'Yes, everyone knows Dougie. He's attending a meeting in the library but he shouldn't be much longer,' she volunteered. Angel was thankful that she didn't ask her any questions.

Fifteen minutes later, as she looked in the direction of the library, she saw him walking alone. He was talking on his cell phone. Her mouth went dry and her heart leapt about. By now she would've thought she'd have grown accustomed to the effect he had on her, but each time it was like seeing God himself emerging from the clouds. She stood two cars away, pretending to be waiting for someone else. She could now clearly hear him speaking on the phone.

'I'm not gonna make it Craig, I've got two more meetings left then my evenings will be free again. I can't bale out now dude,' he said. She felt like such a traitor but she needed to do this. *What meeting?* She wondered as she stared at him. He looked a lot more mature than before, and even handsomer. It took huge willpower to keep her distance. Hanging up, he opened his car door. Then he looked up and caught her staring at him. For a moment their eyes locked.

Chapter 28

She wished for a moment that she had a car in which to hide–as well as to follow him home. Regaining her grip on reality, she realised it was time to get back herself. She decided to walk; she needed the exercise and the cool wind would do her mind good.

A block from the B&B, she could see Jake in the distance on his bicycle, clutching a bouquet of roses in his hand. She couldn't help a sudden shout of laughter as he almost fell off his bicycle trying to juggle the roses and still cross the street. *Lord I am so happy that he has come to his senses and realised that he has an amazing wife. I hope that Belle brings them even closer together,* she thought.

Walking through the door minutes later, she saw the roses had already been put in a vase. Dayna was looking happy for the first time. She tried to tip-toe past them to her room but they stopped her in her tracks. 'Belle, come on over, we want to ask you something,' Dayna called softly. Angel walked over to them. Dayna was holding Belle in her arms, and Angel rubbed her soft, velvety cheeks. 'We were wondering if you would like to have dinner with us on Saturday night. We will have a few friends over and you're the only guest from the B&B that we're inviting. We'd love to have you join us,' Dayna said.

Angel was touched by their kind gesture. 'Thank you so much, it means a lot to me,' she said timidly, 'but unfortunately

I will be leaving on Friday.'

'That's too bad. We've really enjoyed having you with us and you've brought so much peace into this place, it feels like we've known you for a long time,' Dayna said. Jake nodded in agreement. They chatted for a while longer, then Angel excused herself. *Lord, it is thanks to You working through me that I bring about this peace in people's lives. I never want that to end Lord. Use me and never let me go.*

Easter Sunday was a few days away and Angel woke up the next morning with thoughts of spoiling Katie with Easter eggs of every kind. She walked over to Bread 'n Bake where she knew there would be a vast variety to choose from. Grabbing a basket, she threw in a few items and could not decide which egg to get for Katie. Then out of nowhere, she heard a man's voice beside her.

'Fancy seeing you here again. I've seen you around a few times. My name is Craig,' he said, holding his hand out to shake hers. He was the last person she had expected to see, let alone have a conversation with. *This isn't part of the plan,* she thought, panicked. She scouted around for Doug.

'Yes, I remember seeing you as well. My name's Belle,' she said with a little stab of dismay in her soft French accent. Craig was also deciding on the Easter eggs, or so it appeared. 'So, where's your friend today?' she asked, not sure if it was the appropriate question. But the need to know was beyond her.

'You mean Dougie. Yes, if I remember correctly you were checking him out that day,' he said teasingly. Angel's face felt like it was steaming. She did not reply. 'Dougie has a girlfriend by the way, so you will have to settle for me,' he chuckled, making a debonair bow. They both giggled. Then it struck her hard that he had just mentioned he had a girlfriend. Trying not to look too obvious, she probed him on a little further.

'Well, I could have guessed that much,' she said, grabbing Easter eggs of any kind and filling her basket. 'One seldom finds good looking men that are single,' she continued, then blushed even more when she realised what she had said. Craig didn't miss a beat.

'I'm good looking AND single,' he said, truly enjoying the game. He had diligently set out to make himself wanted and needed, but not in a devious way. 'I remained single knowing that I would meet a French girl, in a bakery, sooner or later,' he added. She was tickled by his sense of humour and giggled in spite of herself.

'Craig, it was great meeting you…' she said, resolving to end the conversation before she got into hot water.

'So, why don't you join us one evening. I'm sure I can organise your Dougie to be there. But no promises, hey, 'cos he's committed to this girl.' Again she tried hard not to seem fazed. Inside she was burning to find out more about the girl. *Lord, is that girl me or am I way over the top with false hope?*

'Maybe next time,' she stalled. She tried to walk on but he followed her.

'Well we will be at Lord Charles on Friday night if you decide to join us,' he said in parting.

'Sure, I'll think about it. Thanks,' she said. Her heart raced as she smiled and waved him goodbye. How she would love to go... but she wouldn't dare, least of all on her own. She quickly went to the next aisle, threw out the eggs that she didn't want and rushed to the till.

Angel stopped over at a few other shops but her mind was clearly not on shopping. *Angel, Doug has a girl and it may not be you,* a voice kept warning her but she needed confirmation. She knew Faith would be able to help.

'Angel, how are you doing?' she asked, picking up the

phone. Angel was thrilled to hear her voice and told Faith everything from bumping into Craig to his asking her to go clubbing with them.

'That sounds exciting, I think you should go!' Faith said. Angel couldn't believe how daring Faith was telling her to be.

'I could never do that, Faith,' she protested. 'What would I do if Doug started talking to me? My so-called French accent would not work too well under duress.' Faith laughed out loud and it got her laughing too.

'You're right Angel, I don't think it would work to your advantage. But I have a better idea. Don't forget that Lord Charles forms part of the Athlone Hotel. So there's nothing to stop the two of us from having a sundowner in the formal lounge, if you know what I mean,' Faith suggested, giggling. The pitter-patter of Angel's heart started again; Faith just ignited the butterflies that had gone to sleep.

'You mean we should be spies?' she wavered.

Faith laughed even louder. 'I wouldn't call it spying, that sounds bad. It's good clean fun for the last time before you become Angel again,' Faith said.

This time it was Angel's turn to giggle like a naughty schoolgirl. 'Faith you are the best. Why didn't I think of that? We can get a perfect view of them walking in and hanging about.' Suddenly this crazy venture didn't sound so ridiculous after all. 'Would you really do that with me?' she asked, wondering if it wasn't too much to ask of Faith.

'Of course I would do that for you Angel. I'm due for a night out anyway. It's been a while and my parents can see to Katie that night, I will arrange it.'

'Thank you Faith, from the bottom of my heart,' Angel said, tears burning her eyelids.

'I will fetch you from the main bus stop in First Avenue on Friday afternoon, then you can spend the night at my house.

Katie won't be home till late Saturday afternoon,' Faith rattled on, shifting into organising mode. It sounded like the perfect plan. When Angel hung up, she felt an intense connection with Faith. She was the most selfless person she had met in a long time. She knew she was exceptionally fortunate to have such a dedicated and devoted friend. Suddenly, she could not wait for Friday night to come. She would prepare her heart if she should see Doug walk in with a girl at his side.

Her spirits high, the thought of shopping became interesting again. She wandered from shop to shop making sure each and every person close to her heart had a souvenir from her so-called 'holiday'. Angel loved spoiling people. For Belle, she found a beautiful silver jewellery box in the shape of a heart. It wasn't fancy but it looked sentimental. She would ask Dayna to explain to Belle how she got her name one day, and this would be something she could keep as a souvenir.

As she walked back home, thoughts of Jo flooded her mind. She missed her more so today than any other day. She knew that Jo had been right when she had foreseen her blessings coming in tenfold. Arriving back at the B&B, she took her time wrapping each present individually with a special message attached. She may not have had the luxury of a big family or many friends, but the few she did have in her life brought her great joy. Her cell phone then vibrated with a message from Crystal.

'So glad you're coming home soon. Can't wait to see you at work on Monday, it hasn't been the same without you. Please give me a call,' it read.

'I'm counting the hours Crys, I've missed you more than you'll ever know,' Angel replied immediately.

Two days went by and Angel enjoyed moments spent with Belle and Dayna. She caught up on TV soapies and enjoyed sleeping in till late every morning. There was no doubt that she was fully rested and ready to face life's journey as Angel again. Friday came and it was time for Angel to say goodbye to Dayna. They exchanged numbers and hugged one another goodbye.

'Thank you for Belle's lovely gift. I will tell her all about you and how you saved our lives,' Dayna said, her voice croaking. Angel changed the subject and promised to come and visit again.

Sitting with her heavy luggage at the bus stop on First Avenue, Angel sat waiting for Faith to fetch her. It had been a wonderful, soul-searching holiday. Her mind and soul were renewed and she had the strength of an army of soldiers to face whatever came her way.

Chapter 29

*A*rriving at Faith's house, she felt the void as soon as they walked into the house. She missed Katie's little arms around her legs and she longed to hold her against her heart. Three weeks had felt like forever. Faith could read her mind and led her to the lounge. They sat for a while before getting ready for their night out. Looking at Faith, Angel wondered how she had possibly managed to survive the heartache after the fire. She walked around the lounge looking at photos of the three of them—once a perfect family. She and Faith had a common bond: they had lost the most important people in their lives and were both left with very little. Yet they had each other.

'Angel, don't you think he was handsome?' Faith asked, passing her a photograph of her beloved Keith.

'Yes he was... and he's a hero, Faith. Katie will carry that in her heart forever, her Daddy the Hero.'

Faith smiled and then burst into a deep sob. Angel could not console her enough. She let out all her emotions and told her every detail of the sad event until Angel too began to cry. It was a good thing that Katie was out. 'I miss Katie too, Angel,' Faith sobbed. 'I need my little girl to talk to me, to tell me when she's happy and when she's sad, or if she had a bad day at school or if....'

But Faith's sobs just got worse. *Lord, please help me to be strong for Faith. What do I say to her Lord? Put the right words into my mouth please.* Then with a sense of total calm and enormous strength, Angel turned to face Faith. 'Katie will speak again Faith. Let us both declare this now together. God did not rescue her from the fire to live a life of silence. He has huge plans for her and she will talk to you and tell you in person how much she loves you.'

Lord, is that true? Is that coming from You? A voice in her head whispered, *'Trust me Beloved.'*

They both wiped their tears and Faith got up to pour two glasses of wine. 'Whenever I got flustered about anything, Keith would always pour us a glass of wine. So here's to a good night out, just the two of us,' said Faith as they clicked their glasses together.

'Yes, let's get ready for a night well deserved,' echoed Angel, getting up to touch up her makeup.

'Angel, I've been meaning to ask, how are you enjoying Belle?' Faith asked as she watched Angel apply her lipstick.

'Faith, I'd go back to Angel in a flash for more reasons than one,' she said without hesitation. Faith grinned.

'It was nice meeting Belle but I miss Angel,' she agreed as they walked out the door. It was a beautiful evening and a full moon lit up the night sky. Couples were walking the streets hand in hand, and children were still playing outdoors. It was a fifteen minute drive to Athlone Hotel and a catchy tune was playing on the radio. It was the makings of a perfect evening and Angel would not allow doubt to spoil it. There was a buzz of people streaming in and out of Lord Charles, which was surprising as they'd arrived there early. They sat on a huge sofa next to a fireplace, directly opposite the entrance to Lord Charles. It was perfect and no-one would think to even look in their direction. They put their feet up and ordered a tall cocktail each. Angel's eyes did not leave the entrance door whilst they chatted.

An hour later, Angel caught sight of Craig and the same girl he had walked out with at the varsity. Behind him were two other guys and their partners, and then Colin–Crystal's Colin. Laughter bubbled up in Angel at the absurdity of the situation, and she was unable to suppress it.

'Faith we have some action. They've arrived but I don't see Doug,' she said in a low voice. A part of her was disappointed but she kept her eye on them as she described to Faith who each person was. Colin must have hugged at least five women in a space of ten minutes. Angel stared as he walked off outside with a brunette. The others all stood around the entrance for a while before going inside. Faith and Angel felt like two naughty school girls in the corner. Then out of the dark, like a mystical illusion, she saw Doug walking towards the door. His hands were in his pockets and he had no-one at his side. Faith could see the sudden colour in her cheeks.

'Faith, there he is! There's Doug!' she said, her eyes dancing.

'Sssh, let's sit back calmly, we can't let them spot us,' Faith reminded her, just as excited as Angel. The friends all met up at the door and one by one they walked in. The two women continued to sip their cocktails and chat about all sorts. Angel's eyes were fixed on the door. After a while she saw Colin coming out and walking towards his car with another girl. Angel carefully scrutinised him and could see no trace of guilt.

'I just want to go over there and smack that man 'til he is black and blue. He deserves each and every bruise he has handed out...'

The seriousness of her tone alarmed Faith. 'Are you going to tell Crystal what you saw?' she asked.

Angel's eyes were deep, serious. 'Yes I will! Even if I

stand a chance of jeopardising our friendship, she needs to know.' Feeling hot and flustered, Angel got up to get some air. She excused herself and walked over to the main double door of the hotel. She looked up at the moon and a breeze swept over her face as if it were speaking to her. Her thoughts were racing. *What will life be like back home next week? Will I return to my mundane routine or will I have Doug to bring meaning to my life?*

She looked back to see Faith walking towards the ladies' room. She went down two steps until she was directly beneath the moon. She stood for a long moment in the moonlight with her head bowed, reluctant to leave its peaceful presence. Then she tilted her head back so that the moonlight shone over her face.

Just then Doug walked past. Seeing her standing with her head tilted back and her eyes closed, he saw a peace in her face that he had never felt–a peace for which he hungered and searched. 'You shouldn't be out here alone at this time of the night,' he said to her when he came to his senses. She jumped at the sound of his voice and looked ready to faint when she saw him. For the first time in her life, she was lost for words. She simply froze and quickly looked away. *Lord, what do I do? He cannot see me. Come to my rescue Lord.*

Giving her a slightly embarrassed smile, he moved on towards another man who had waved in the distance. Out of the corner of her eye, she saw his gaze return to her. Alarm spread through Angel. This was not like her. Not at all. *Lord, I cannot fake my identity anymore. This is NOT who I am Lord.*

Something about this girl intrigued Doug. Perhaps it was the combination of innocence and serenity. Conscious of Doug's eye on her, Angel turned and walked back inside, going straight past Faith so as not to make it obvious. On entering the ladies' room, she phoned Faith from her cell phone.

'Angel, did you just walk right past me? Where are you?' Faith replied, perplexed.

'Long story Faith, but we have to go. Meet me at the car.' She hung up, leaving Faith very intrigued. Angel waited at the car until Faith came running towards her.

'Angel are you okay?' she asked quizzically.

With that, Angel burst into a fit of laughter. 'Faith, Doug spoke to me outside, one on one!' Faith's expression was priceless.

'No way, he didn't! Did he really?' By now the two of them were squealing and giggling like two naughty pranksters. Their laughter echoed in the parking lot and the moonlight revealed the tears of laughter streaming down their cheeks.

'Faith, why did he look at me? I am beautiful remember... do you think he was trying to hit on me?' Before Faith could reply, Angel saw Doug coming towards the cars. She clapped her hand over Faith's mouth and dropped to her knees, pulling Faith down with her. It was a sight to behold. They heard the footsteps getting closer. Then his phone rang and they nearly jumped out of their skins.

'Howzit,' they heard him say clearly. 'I tried looking for you to tell you I'm leaving.' They could see him resting his back against his car. 'Not my scene tonight buddy but we can meet up for a gaming session tomorrow. AA meetings are finished now, so I've got my evenings back after three weeks.' They continued to listen, both wide eyed and taking it all in. 'Yeah, just hope she will see a changed me,' he said.

Angel went dead to the rest of his conversation. In the faint light, she noticed the look of gloom on his face and knew she must reassure him *now*. She was about to stand up and run to him when Faith managed to grab her dress just in time. 'No Angel!' she hissed. Then they heard him get into the car and drive away. Quite suddenly she saw everything with vivid clarity.

'Faith, oh Faith… oh… is AA what I think it is, tell me Faith…'

Faith's radiant smile widened. 'Yes my darling friend, AA is Alcoholics Anonymous and he is doing it for you… for Angel, not for Belle.' They threw their arms around one another as tears of joy trickled down their faces. *Lord, You did it again. You are blessing me daily but this is by far the greatest blessing I could ever receive. Thank you Father God, thank you, thank you!*

Arriving back home, they sat chatting over a cup of coffee. 'Thank you for the greatest evening of my life Faith,' said an elated Angel.

'We did have fun, didn't we?' her friend replied, and they both started to laugh all over again as they thought of themselves on their knees in the parking lot.

'I think we would make good detectives,' Angel joked. 'You would make a good partner in crime.'

'You nearly gave it away you chop,' Faith giggled.

'You've got no idea how hard it was not to run into his arms, Faith.'

'Oh yes I do,' Faith replied. 'I was once there.'

As midnight struck, they both went off to bed. It had been such an eventful day that Angel did not have to feign tiredness tonight. She fell asleep thinking about the new life awaiting her back home.

Chapter 30

The next morning, Angel was awoken by Faith standing beside her with a tray of coffee and rusks. It had been a long time since someone had woken her up with coffee in bed, and the memory of Jo came to mind. 'Thank you Faith. These are my favourite rusks too.'

'You're welcome Angel. So... was Katie's bed comfortable?'

Angel smiled as she pictured Katie lying beside her. 'I bet you must be happy to have her back today.'

'Oh yes, she is all I have and I cannot function without her,' Faith confessed.

'Be sure to tell her that I will see her in two more sleeps,' Angel reminded her, longing to see her little friend. Angel stayed on for a while longer after breakfast, then Faith took her to the salon en route to fetch Katie. *Lord, I know another action-packed moment awaits me now with Crystal. This is not easy but it's the last time, so I will remain calm and do as You will.*

At the Salon she sat waiting for Liz, who was probably attending to Crystal. She paged through a magazine, listening to the soft background music. Just then, the door opened and Crystal walked in. *Lord, my heart cannot take these unexpected jolts each time. I do not understand–Crystal's appointment was meant to be before mine.*

I have a plan Beloved. Angel semi-covered her face with the magazine as Crystal walked in chewing her customary gum. Noticing Angel, she said, 'I believe Liz is an hour behind. So you must be after me, is that right?'

Angel relied on her French accent to be flawless. 'Ah yes, my appointment was meant to be at twelve.'

'Yeah, now I'm going in at twelve,' she said, giggling as she grabbed a magazine.

'I like your shoes,' she said, staring at Angel's stilettos.

'Thanks' was all Angel could say, hoping she could just be quiet and read her magazine.

'I like the accent too, where are you from?' Angel shifted in her seat and cleared her throat.

'Ah, I'm from Paris. So where do you work?' she asked trying to change the subject.

'I'm a financial consultant at United Bank,' she said, chewing at her gum vivaciously.

This was her moment of truth. 'Yeah… now I recognise you. I've been to your work. The other lady served me, I can't remember her name now... you know, the sweet, thin girl with the pale face.'

Crystal smiled. 'Yeah that's Angel. Sweet doesn't describe it, more like angelic.' Angel's heart felt like it had turned into a blob of melted wax. 'That's right, it was Angel. So is it just the two of you consultants?' she asked, trying to make small talk.

'Yes, it's a small branch so two consultants is ample.' Then they sat quietly until Crystal's phone rang.

'Hi, yes I'm having a wax and manicure, I told you so when I left.' Angel tried to calm the wild beating of her heart. 'No Colin, I won't hurry up. Just cook yourself something,' she said and promptly hung up on him.

'Oh dear, boyfriend problems?' Angel asked boldly.

'Yeah, little does he know that his days are numbered.' Angel got such a fright that she choked on her saliva. She coughed until she felt she could cough no more. 'Are you okay? You look like you've seen a ghost,' she said. Angel casually took it in her stride, picking up her magazine that had fallen off her lap.

'Yes, I'm fine. So you were saying his days are numbered. Wow I'm sorry to hear that,' she said, trying to look apologetic. Meanwhile she could've burst at the seams in sheer glory.

'Yeah, it took me a long time to decide but when my best friend is back, I'm gonna pluck up the courage with her help.' Angel could not take another moment of unexpressed emotion.

'Yes, best friends are good for that kind of thing. I also have a best friend I couldn't live without,' she said casually, pretending to be fixated in a story in the mag.

'So what's Paris like?' she asked. Angel's hands perspired so much that she needed to wipe them dry. *Lord, what do I do? What do I tell her about a country I've never visited in my life?*

'Ah... well, the Eiffel Tower is a must if ever you come visit...' Just then Liz opened the door and Crystal was ready to waltz in.

'Anyhow, say hi to Paris for me,' she said as they closed the door behind them. Angel exhaled. She realised she'd been holding her breath for way too long. *Phew, thank you Lord. I am so glad this was the last time.*

On the bus trip back home, Angel had only one desire: to rip off her wig and be herself again. She got off at the mall two blocks from home. In the ladies' restroom, she locked herself in a cubicle and stripped off her wig. She shoved it into her bag and gave her hair a good brush. Then she took off her heels and reached in her bag for her beach sandals. It felt so good. She then went over to the basin and was thankful that she was alone. Wiping off her make-up, she slowly saw Angel come back to life. She looked in the mirror and Jo's words came back loud and clear. *One day a man will love you for who you are on the inside Angel.*

Thank you Lord, for the experience of a lifetime. It served its purpose. I am happy with ME Lord, not anybody else. And I know that I am loved for who I am. She could feel tears welling up in her eyes... but this was not the time to cry. Walking back with her luggage, she felt as free as a bird. And if the strongest gale-force winds were to blow, she needn't worry to hold down her hair.

Walking into the tearoom down the road, she bought a tin of cat food. She chose the most expensive and delicious one, full of gravy. 'Angel, where have you been all this time? I worried sick about you,' said the owner of the shop. He had never spoken to her before and she did not even know his name. All he did was nod at her each time she came into the shop.

'Ah... thank you so much. I was on holiday but it's good to be back home,' she replied, smiling. Even the shop owner cares, she thought as she skipped her way home. Her road was full of buzz as usual as she approached Jo's home–her home. She went straight over to her neighbour to fetch Mimi. He gave Angel a big hug and told her that it hadn't been the same without her.

'Mimi is probably sleeping in your house. She only comes here to eat and then goes back each time,' he said, grinning. Angel thanked him warmly. She unlocked the door to her house and immediately Mimi sat up and looked at her.

'Mimi, mommy's home!' she squealed as she picked her up and held her to her cheeks. If ever a cat could smile, Mimi was grinning all over her face now. Angel immediately

156

opened the tin and watched in delight as she licked the bowl clean. Without further ado she threw herself on the couch and fell into a deep sleep with Mimi snug at her side.

The loud music and revving of a car engine next door woke her with a jolt. It was two in the morning. Lying awake, she was suddenly aware of every sound that seemed unusual. She got up and walked through the house–a defence mechanism induced by her childhood. She recalled Granny Jo walking around with a torch in the night. And now, living alone at home, Angel often got up to check. One day she would have a man at her side to hold the torch. ***Do not fear Beloved, you are never alone.***

The next morning, Angel had one aim: to phone Crystal. She had not looked at the time before dialling her number and the phone rang for a long time before Crystal answered. 'Hello?' came a groggy reply.

Angel was bursting with joy at finally being able to speak to her. 'Crys, its Angel. I'm back!' Silence on the other end. Then came Crystal's voice in a mere whisper.

'Angel, do you realise it is five on a Sunday morning?'

Angel looked at the wall clock. 'Oops sorry, but I missed you, I couldn't wait any longer,' she said apologetically. She was on her second cup of coffee already.

'Man, I missed you too in a big way. Tell me all about your holiday tomorrow at work okay? Now can I go back to bed?'

That was so typical of Crystal that Angel laughed. 'Yes you may. Oh and Crys, guess what?' Crystal waited with eyes half shut. 'I love you,' said Angel, then said goodbye. Crystal was awake then and could not wait for the next day to tell her how much she had missed her.

Chapter 31

*T*hat night, on turning out the lights and tucking herself into bed, she was tempted to message Doug. She wanted him to know that she was back home. But he already knew. *Tomorrow Angel he will come and visit you of his own accord. Be patient just a little while longer*, she told herself. Angel said her prayers and asked God to strengthen her for the day ahead.

The sound of the alarm clock was a shock to her system the next morning. It had been a while since she had been awoken in such a manner. She jumped out of bed and was happy simply to wash her face and apply a stroke of lipstick. Her hair framed her face attractively and Crystal would be pleased at the life she had put back into it. Grabbing her bag and wallet, she realised she had totally overspent on her holiday. She would need to scrimp and scrape for a while to build up her savings again.

She grabbed her scooter which had collected dust in the garage and wiped it down with a cloth. The red gloss shone through, triggering flashbacks of Doug's red scooter. Driving off into the sunshine, her wings felt renewed and strong. She breathed the fresh air deep into her lungs. *This is going to be a good day,* she thought.

Mr Reid welcomed her back and had a pile of work ready for her on her desk. *Some welcoming that was*, she thought; but she was ready to face the mountain of work that undoubtedly lay ahead. She grabbed her cup of coffee and waited patiently for Crys to arrive. By eight she had already managed to get a quarter way through her papers.

Finding it strange that Crystal had still not arrived, Angel sent her a message from her cell: 'Hey where are you? Your coffee is getting cold. Hurry your steps and get your butt over here please.' Angel continued with her work until the first customers started piling in. She would not manage without Crystal and wondered what could be keeping her.

Then Mr Reid came over to her. 'Any idea why Crystal would be late this morning?' he asked. Angel could sense trouble–a knot was forming in her stomach. Crystal would never miss work today of all days; she had been so excited to see Angel.

'Mr Reid, I will quickly make a phone call and let you know.' She tried Crystal's number again but it just rang. Something was wrong. She wished she had taken down Crystal's mom's number for the main house. Mr Reid was apologising to the customers for the wait. She walked over to him, praying that he would be understanding. 'Uh… uh, Mr Reid, I really need to leave. Something is wrong and I need to go and see that Crystal is okay.' She had never seen him angry before.

'What are you contemplating, Angel?' he asked, pushing her aside.

'Sir, I may be wrong–for which I sincerely apologise–but I know that Crystal is in trouble and she needs me right now. I will make it up to you Mr Reid, I promise.' Without waiting for his approval, she turned to walk away. *Lord, my first day back at work and this happens. Please don't let me lose my job, I simply cannot lose my job Lord.*

She grabbed her helmet and bag and leaped onto her scooter, her heart pounding in fear. *Lord, I have the same feeling as I had with Dayna,* she prayed. *Please save Crystal, I just know she is in trouble. Send me there in time again Lord, anything is possible with You.* She took the shortcut at full throttle. She didn't like this route–it was creepy and deserted–but today she was fearless. God was beside her and she knew it. All she wanted was to find Crystal unharmed.

She could see Colin's car in the driveway and her heart dropped. This was serious. Parking her bike on the verge, she tiptoed up the driveway and tried the door of Crystal's cottage. It was locked, and so were the windows. But the curtains in the front bay window were open, and Angel could see Colin standing over Crystal with his hands on his hips. Angel saw a crushed look on Crystal's face. Then she heard her speak in a voice she'd never heard her use before. It was full of cold, steely fury. 'I hate you. Get out of my life,' she said, looking straight at him.

His swift temper rose at her imperious tone. Colin swore at her and a tremor ran through Angel's body. 'If you scream, I swear I will hurt you like never before,' he said menacingly as he clamped his hand around Crystal's wrist. Angel swallowed her tears, forcing herself not to lose control. Before she could move, she saw him throw her across the room. She hit her head on the coffee table and landed flat on her back. She looked too shocked to react, and Colin felt the thrill of his power over her.

Gulping back the knot in her throat, she knew she had no time to waste if she wanted to save Crys. With a brick from the edge of the path, she smashed the window and shouted at the top of her voice, 'Leave her alone or I will phone the police!'

Colin turned and stared at Angel without emotion. She knew she had struck a chord of fear in him. With adrenaline pumping through her veins, she climbed through the low window and ran towards Crystal who was lying on the floor. Dread swept through her chest as Colin turned around like a raging bull. Taking a step back, she stumbled over a rug and hit the wall in the corner. 'You coward!' she yelled, her blood boiling.

He took a step forward and grabbed her by her collar. She pushed him back and this infuriated him. He lifted his hand and was ready to hit her when Crystal screamed and threw a glass at him. 'Dad, help us!' she screamed as she heard a car in the driveway.

Colin stared at her for a split second, then jumped through the window and ran down the driveway. Blood poured from the cut on Crystal's temple, running over her eye and down her cheek. Consumed with pain, she squinted her eyes against the sunlight that was streaming through the window. The room shifted out of focus as she reached to steady herself on a chair.

Picking herself up from the floor, Angel ran over to Crys and embraced her. As if spellbound, they hung onto each other while a storm of emotion raged within. Just then Crystal's parents came to the window and were appalled at the sight. Crystal's mom worried like a mother hen over her chick, and rightfully so. Crystal was a mess. Her dad phoned the police then leaped into his car–he was furious and bent on finding Colin.

Arriving at the hospital, Crystal did not want to let go of Angel's hand. 'Thank you Angel, you saved my life. I think this time he would have killed me.'

Angel tried to be strong and caressed her face. 'Try to sleep Crystal. He won't ever hurt you again. I need to get back to work before Mr Reid fires both of us.' They both giggled. She walked out of the hospital feeling like she had run a marathon. How would she find the energy to attend to customers after an incident like this? But there were only four hours left of the day, and with God's strength she knew she'd manage.

Chapter 32

*M*r Reid called her into the office. She briefly told him about Crystal's relationship with Colin and how he was no longer in her life. He applauded her for rescuing Crystal and told Angel he would bring back the lady who had temped for her while she was away. There was no hurry for Crystal to come back.

Angel worked hard all afternoon, battling at times to keep her eyes open. She had promised Katie a visit this afternoon and could never let her down. According to little Katie, there were no more sleeps. As the clock struck four, Angel packed up and took a bus to Crystal's to pick up her scooter. When she got home, she had just enough time to take a quick shower, grab the souvenirs and Easter eggs, and set off again. Faith had messaged her that Katie was counting the minutes.

Coasting up to Faith's as quietly as she could, she saw little Katie waiting for her on the front steps of the house. She realised she was just as excited as Katie. Then Faith came out and they both waited cross-legged on the steps for her. Killing the motor, Angel ducked and slowly rolled up to the gate. Then she stood up, making herself clearly visible. Angel wished someone could have captured the scene that followed on video. It was too precious for words.

Katie looked up and she jumped up screaming 'Mommy,

Angel's back, Mommy look!' It felt as if time stood still for a moment. Faith and Angel's expression of shock were indescribable. Katie ran down the stairs and jumped into Angel's arms. 'Angel, I missed you,' she cried. Angel threw her up in the air with tears streaming down her face.

'Katie, you can talk! You just spoke to me Katie! Thank you my darling, thank you so much for missing me,' Angel wept. She kissed her over and over again.

Faith had fallen to her knees with her hands raised to heaven. 'Thank you God for sending your Angel.'

The three of them held one another for what felt like a lifetime. Then Angel put Katie down and said she had a surprise for her. 'What did you buy for me Angel?' Her sweet little voice was music to her ears. Faith came from behind and wrapped her arms around Angel. She listened attentively at the conversation between Angel and Katie.

'Angel, why did you leave?' Angel felt like her heart was being squeezed.

'I don't know darling, there are many things in life we don't understand. What we do know is that God loves us.' A couple of months ago she might not have been able to give the same response. Indeed God had been working to heal her wounded spirit.

They kept throwing questions at Katie, and they couldn't get enough of the joy of hearing her speak. It started to get dark and they went inside. Katie ran around as if someone had wound her up. 'Mommy, why can't I fly like a bird?' she asked.

'Because we are human beings and we don't have wings,' Faith replied with a smile that melted Angel's heart.

As Katie ran into the kitchen, Angel pulled at Faith's arm. 'Do you know why she asked that question, Faith?' Faith remained quiet. 'It's because she has been set free.

When one's burdens lift, one inevitably wants to fly,' Angel explained as she stroked Faith's arm to reassure her.

'You are so right Angel. Look at the excitement in her. I've never seen her like this.' They sat and watched her until it was time for Angel to go. She had not given Doug a second thought the entire evening and felt guilty now.

'I have to go,' she whispered to Faith.

But Katie heard her loud and clear. 'No Angel, please stay,' she pleaded. As if afraid that she would wake up to a silent child again tomorrow, Faith offered for Angel to sleep over.

Looking at her watch, Angel wondered if Doug would visit her tonight. 'Alright, I'll stay.' It took huge courage to make that decision as Katie looked at her with those puppy dog eyes.

'Yipee, I knew you would!' she shrieked and off she skipped again.

After borrowing a pair of pyjamas and a dress for the next day, Angel went upstairs to have a shower. She stood in the shower with her head tilted back as the hot water pelted down on her. *I need to get through this day,* she told herself. Swallowing hard, she took a firm grip on her emotions. *Enjoy this day for what it is, Angel. And as for tomorrow, don't dwell on what it might be.*

Grabbing her gown, she walked over to Katie's room. *Crystal–I need to phone her,* she remembered. Sinking into a chair next to the bed, she dialled her number. Crystal answered promptly. 'It's me, just checking on you. How are you feeling?' Angel asked.

After a few seconds of silence Crystal replied. 'I'm feeling great Angel, don't worry about me.' Crystal was a proud person and one could never really tell what went on inside her heart and mind. It didn't take much insight on

Angel's part to realise she was lying. *You may fool us but you'll never fool God*, she said silently, asking God to set her free of those chains. *In MY time Beloved*, she was certain she heard him say.

'Stay home tomorrow and rest, and I will stop by to see you after work,' she told Crystal. Then she hung up and threw her head back. Sleep would not be a battle tonight. Just then Katie came in and Faith tucked her into bed.

'Please can you sleep next to me tonight Angel?' Katie asked. Angel nodded, smiling. Just as they were about to walk out, they heard Katie call. Faith put her head in the door. 'I love you mommy,' she said and Faith went leaping back in. Angel left them to kiss and cuddle. Minutes later, Faith joined her in the lounge.

'I told you she would speak again and I also told you that she would tell you in person how much she loves you,' Angel reminded her. Faith just stared at her as if she was looking into her soul.

'Angel have I ever told you that your name applies? You really have touched our lives like an angel.'

Grinning, Angel replied, 'And have I ever told you that your name applies too? You believed and your dream was fulfilled.'

They both hugged one another and carried their tired legs to bed. Lying beside Katie, she took her little hand in hers and fell asleep just the way Granny Jo had held her hand as a little girl.

Chapter 33

The next morning she was awoken by the sound of a fluffy panda asking Katie her name.

Katie replied to each and every question the panda asked her. Angel thought back to the miracle that had taken place the previous night. She could watch Katie at play for hours on end and not grow weary doing so. Just then Faith walked in with her usual tray of homemade rusks and creamy coffee. She signalled to Angel with movements of her eye as if to ask: 'Is she still speaking today?' Angel chuckled and nodded.

Then, as if to prove a point, Katie looked up at her mother and asked, 'Mommy, can we go shopping today?'

Faith had waited a whole year for those very words. 'Yes my darling, we will spend all day together doing whatever you want.' Faith went over and held her close to her heart.

Moments later, Angel was ready to leave. Turning to Katie, she said, 'I will see you in a few days. I won't be gone for long this time okay?' Katie nodded with a happy face. They waved her goodbye as she drove off on her scooter. It was a long, drawn out day. She attended to many customers and was tired of smiling. All she wanted to do was go home to Mimi and her bed. On leaving, she could see Craig in the distance but was too tired emotionally and physically to worry about what he said or did. Driving down her road, she could see that her wild neighbours had had a party of some kind. Beer cans littered the verge and serviettes were flying about in the wind. A few people she recognised were lying on the lawn and waved at her as she drove past. Politely she waved back. She locked her scooter in the garage and fled inside.

At the front door she stopped in her tracks. There at her feet was a bouquet of thirteen beautiful red roses–one rose for each year since he had met her. If ever she had an instant awakening, it was there and then. Shakily, she bent down and picked them up. The fragrance was intoxicating. *Oh Doug,* she said to herself, *I'm so sorry I missed you.* She opened the miniature envelope attached and it read: 'Welcome back home Angel. You've been missed. If you can remember who I am, give me a call. I'll be waiting.'

How could I ever forget you, Doug? I never forgot you in thirteen years, I sure wouldn't forget you in three weeks. She fumbled with her keys as her trembling hand opened the door. Reaching for her phone, she dialled his number. Finally she could speak to him for real. There was no more hiding, no more pretending.

As he replied, she went into freeze mode. 'They're beautiful Doug, the roses are beautiful,' she said, trying to calm the tremor in her voice.

'Not as beautiful as you are, Angel,' he said softly. She blushed and could picture him staring at her. For the first time she knew he meant what he said. To him Angel was beautiful and it shocked him to think she thought otherwise of herself.

'I've missed you Doug. I need to see you now, today,' she said confidently.

'I'm on my way, Angel,' he said and then he hung up. Her entire body went into a frenzy. Mimi watched her jump around shouting 'He loves me! He loves me!' She raced to the shower and within minutes she had made herself look gorgeous. Looking in the mirror, she had a chat with herself. *Angel, you may not turn heads but you do touch lives and I like what I see before me. It is plain, simple and uncomplicated.*

She quickly messaged Faith and Crystal: 'I got roses! Doug is coming over tonight. I am so happy, words cannot begin to describe what I feel. Love you lots.' Just then she heard knocking on the door. Her legs could hardly carry her weight, they felt so wobbly. She slowly opened it and stared into his dark eyes.

'I've stopped drinking. I've been dry for three weeks,' he said before she had a chance to speak.

She pulled him in by the shirt. 'I believe you,' she said and held him close to her. They melted in each other's arms. Then he looked down at her, lifted her chin and said the most beautiful words.

'You're the only girl for me and I love you.' Angel's heart soared. For a moment she was speechless and she simply stared into his eyes, her own glistening with tears. He lifted his hand and wiped one that had escaped. 'There I've said it. Now you know how much I care. I love everything about you–your smile, your gentle heart, your independence... and your honesty.'

'I love you too Doug. And I have for the past thirteen years,' she smiled through her tears.

Leaning down, Doug pulled her towards him and kissed her with all the love he had stored for a lifetime. She could almost hear Jo's voice: *Love always finds a way Angel.*

Lessons In Life ...

A Word From The Author

In the middle of difficulty, lies opportunity.
Albert Einstein

Angel did not come from a wealthy home, but she was never deprived of happiness or success. No matter what our financial circumstances are, we can be just as happy and successful. Often we hear children say, "When I grow up I will make sure my child will not be as poor as I was". Knowing that we can change our circumstances gives us hope and allows us to set goals. But let's beware of assuming that happiness is tied to material things. The love and care you receive from your loved ones is worth more than gold... and the love that you show the world will bring you true significance. Sometimes starting with little in life makes you a happier and more resourceful person in the end.

Your altitude is determined by your attitude.
Unknown

Angel learned firsthand that she needed to be happy with herself before she could see her true value to others. Being happy with ourselves means showing mercy to ourselves, forgiving ourselves, befriending ourselves and loving ourselves. It is a lifelong journey of constantly making peace with our inner being. We need to be kind to ourselves in order to live life to the fullest. Once we have accepted ourselves, we can then begin to reach out to others.

The big shots are only the little shots who keep shooting.
Christopher Morley

Angel realised along the way that looks can be deceiving. The shimmering surface of a lake that glows in the afternoon sun may look inviting on a hot summer afternoon, yet hidden beneath its surface may be a blanket of sludge. We are often misled by what we see because we merely skim the surface and fail to penetrate the depth. A beautiful woman can be appealing to the eye but she may be a selfish hypocrite who only thinks of her own pleasures. Then there are also those who are not necessarily attractive for various reasons, but who are content in life and make a real difference in the world. It's these people who are the salt of the earth, and who leave their fragrance wherever they go.

Children are the living messages we send to a time we will not see.
Unknown

Angel believed in Katie from the beginning. Katie felt that positive vibe coming from Angel and it made her feel safe and hopeful. Even though she had a loving mother, she may have sensed her worry and sadness. But with Angel she felt the positive assurance that one day she would speak again, in her own time. Feelings and emotions are just as strong in children as they are in adults. We may not understand the intensity of their feelings but emotions are very real to them. It is important that adults are able to communicate and listen to children and teach them that every action leads to a certain feeling or emotion. Actions evoke feelings and those feelings bring about responses. Children are precious: we must love them, hear them, guide them and protect them.

Never violate the sacredness of your individual self respect.
Theodore Parker

Crystal was a victim of abuse, but with Angel's help she was able to break the chains that held her down. Often a victim feels alone and afraid. Anyone can be a victim – young, old, male, female. Being the weaker sex, the majority of victims are women, children and elderly people. It can happen anywhere and even in facilities responsible for their care. By learning the signs and symptoms of abuse and how to act on behalf of the person being abused, you'll not only be helping someone else but strengthening your own defences against abuse in the future.

Abuse takes on many different forms. It can be physical (non-accidental use of force against a person that results in pain or injury), sexual (being in sexual contact with a person without their consent), emotional (verbal abuse, such as being intimidated by yells or threats, humiliation and ridicule, or scapegoating – or non-verbal abuse, such as being ignored, isolated from friends or activities, terrorised or threatened). The abuser has a hold over the abused and brainwashes the victim to believe that it's her/his fault. You can break free from the abuser... help is always available. Don't be afraid, but look up to someone you can trust.

Family is one of nature's masterpieces.
George Santayana

Angel loved and honoured her mother in spite of her bad habit. Many people grow up with parents who love and provide for them and build values into their lives – and they have no trouble honouring them. But there are some that find it hard to bring themselves to honour their parents because they've always felt they couldn't measure up to their expectations. Or perhaps their mother or father have done wrong in their lives and have not set a good example – so they rebel against everything their parents stand for. We all have only one mother and one father, and no matter what our circumstances or upbringing, we must love and honour them. Make peace with yourself and move forward. Life is too short not to – avoid the remorse.

Decide that you want it more than you are afraid of it.
Bill Cosby

Alcoholism (and other forms of substance abuse) brings conflict, anger, unhappiness and a sense of loss into one's life. This goes for both the abuser (Angel's mother, Doug's father and even Colin) and the innocent person living with that person (Angel and Doug as children). Ask yourself: what would improve in my life if I were to stop drinking? The list could be unending. Then ask yourself how much healthier you feel. You will immediately start seeing the benefits. Quitting an addiction needs to happen from within; and with support and unconditional love, one can be saved.

A last word

Lastly, Angel never quit believing. God is real, He exists, He is alive. When you start believing and when you welcome Him into your heart, His miracles begin to show in your life, prayers are answered and you are guided and protected. Everything and anything is possible with God, so why not give Him the glory.

www.ingramcontent.com/pod-product-compliance
Lightning Source LLC
Chambersburg PA
CBHW070036030726
47506CB00003B/768